A CASE of POSSESSION

KJ CHARLES

First published by Samhain Publishing. This revised edition published 2017.

Published by KJC Books

Cover design by Lexiconic Design
Interior design by eB Format
Swirl created by Alvaro_cabrera - Freepik.com
Edited by Anne Scott

Print ISBN: 978-1-9997846-2-1

For Caroline, best of mates. Drink?

One for sorrow
Two for joy
Three for a girl
Four for a boy
Five for silver
Six for gold
Seven for a secret never to be told
Eight for a letter over the sea
Nine for a lover as true as can be

One for sorrow
Two for joy
Three for a girl
Four for a boy
Five for rich
Six for poor
Seven for a bitch
Eight for a whore
Nine for a funeral
Ten for a dance
Eleven for England
Twelve for France

CHAPTER ONE

On a hot summer's night, in a small, bare clerk's room in Limehouse, a few streets from the stench of the river and three doors down from an opium den, Lucien Vaudrey, the Earl Crane, was checking lading bills. This was not his preferred way to spend an evening, but since his preferences hadn't been consulted, and the work needed to be done, he was doing it.

He went through the bills with the jaundiced eye of a China trader, asking himself not whether he had been stolen from, but where the theft had occurred. If he couldn't find it, that would suggest his factor back home in Shanghai was either cleverer or more honest than he had thought, and Crane didn't think he was particularly honest.

His iron nib scratched down the paper. It was a functional, cheap pen, like the basic deal desk and the plain, sparse office. There was no evidence of wealth in the room at all, in fact, except for Crane's suit, which had cost more than the house he was sitting in.

As Lucien Vaudrey, trader and occasional smuggler, he had made himself satisfactorily rich, and his unexpected elevation to the peerage had brought him a huge fortune along with the title. He was now one of England's most eligible bachelors, to anyone who didn't know or chose to disregard his reputation in China, and he was this very evening failing to attend three separate soirees at which he could have met perhaps thirty women who would be enthusiastically available for the position of the Countess Crane. On his bureau at home were several dozen more visiting cards, invitations, requests for money, requests for meetings: a thick sheaf of *laissez-passer* to the highest society.

He could have his pick of London's beauties, mix with the best people, assert his place in the top few hundred of the Upper Ten Thousand, claim the social status of which many people dreamed and for which some would sacrifice everything. He could have all that if he lifted a finger, and if someone held a gun to his head to make him do it.

Crane had spent his entire adult life in Shanghai, cheek by jowl with smugglers, prostitutes, gamblers, killers, traders, drinkers, shamans, painters, corrupt officials, slumming mandarins, poets, opium eaters, and other such scum, and he loved that sweaty, vivid, intoxicated world. Polite soirees and elegant dinners with people whose achievement in life began and ended with birth held no appeal at all.

So he declined, or ignored, the invitations, because in comparison to high society, identifying where someone had shaved his shipment of Szechuan peppercorns was a much more rewarding pursuit.

Not as rewarding as the pursuit of a certain amber-eyed individual whose small, lithe, delightfully yielding body kept him awake at night, but that wasn't an option right now because the little devil had once again vanished off to work.

Stephen's elusiveness was a novelty for Crane, who had always found getting rid of lovers more of a challenge than picking them up, and who had never had a partner who worked harder than himself. His own idleness was the problem, really, since if his days were fuller he would spend less of them wondering what Stephen was up to, but to amend that by setting up a serious business would require a commitment to England that he couldn't bring himself to make. Not when he had a perfectly good trading house in Shanghai, where life was easier, more comfortable, and so much more fun.

There would be no Stephen in Shanghai, of course, but then for all Crane knew to the contrary, he wasn't in London either. He had disappeared two nights ago without a word, and would return as it suited him.

And that was quite reasonable. Stephen was a free man, and one with responsibilities that made Crane's international business look like a casual pastime. They both had work to do, and since Crane had never tolerated lovers who expected him to put aside his business for their entertainment, he was hardly going to make those demands on Stephen's time. It was merely irritating that the boot was so firmly on the other foot, for once; that it was Crane waiting for Stephen to turn up on his own unpredictable schedule, knowing that he would offer no more than a lopsided, provocative smile as explanation for his absence.

Thinking of his lover's irresistible foxy grin led Crane to a moment's consideration of more interesting uses his desk could be put to. He concluded that the damn thing would doubtless fall apart under the stresses he intended to apply as soon as he got his hands on the little so-and-so, and on that thought at last spotted where the factor's well-massaged figures didn't quite work.

Not a bad effort, he reflected, and a nicely judged theft: enough to be worthwhile for the factor, and quite tolerable for Crane as part of a very competently handled bit of business. He nodded, pleased. The man would work out well.

He reached for the next bill, and there was a loud rapping at the door.

That was tiresome, since he was the only person in the building at eight in the evening, so he ignored it. There was another, more persistent knocking. Then a call, through the iron-barred but open casement.

"Vaudrey! Vaudrey! Crane, I mean." The visitor peered through the window. "There you are. *Nong hao*."

"*Nong hao*, Rackham," said Crane, and went to let him in.

Theo Rackham had been something of a friend in China, as another Englishman who preferred local society to expatriates. Rackham was himself a practitioner of magic, though not a powerful one, and it was he who had introduced Crane to Stephen Day a few months ago.

"This is an unexpected pleasure. How are you?"

Rackham didn't answer immediately. He was wandering about the room, peering at the maps tacked on the plastered walls. "This is your office? I must say, I'd have thought you'd have somewhere rather better than this." He sounded almost affronted.

"What's wrong with it?"

"It's in Limehouse."

"I like Limehouse," Crane said. "So do you."

"I don't like it. Nobody could. Filthy place." Crane raised an eyebrow but didn't bother to ask. "Grubby den of thieves and bullies and madmen," Rackham went on. "If I were rich I wouldn't set foot in this cursed part of town."

Then where would you get your opium? Crane enquired mentally. He had noted Rackham's slightly dilated pupils, but since that was a sign of a practitioner using his powers, as well as an opium fiend, and since, in truth, he didn't care, he hadn't passed judgement.

Rackham seemed to be nursing a grudge. "You're rich. Why don't you act like it? Why aren't you at grand parties in the West End instead of slaving away in the Limehouse docks?"

"I do act like it, on occasion. This coat wasn't cut on the Commercial Road. But my business is here, not the City, and certainly not in the West End."

"I don't see why you have a business at all. You don't need any more money." There was a definite note of accusation in Rackham's voice.

Crane shrugged. "Frankly, I'm bored, and I would not be less bored in the West End. I need something to do, and trading is what I'm good at."

"Why don't you go back to China, then?" Rackham demanded. "If you're so bored with England, why are you still here?"

"Legal business. My father left his affairs in the devil of a state. It's taking forever to resolve, and now I've got distant cousins popping up out of the woodwork demanding their cut. Why do you care?"

"I don't." Rackham scuffed a worn leather toe against the skirting board. "I suppose there's been no recurrence of your troubles?"

"You mean the matter in spring? No. That's all resolved."

"Day dealt with it."

"He did."

Crane had been afflicted by a curse that had killed his father and brother; Rackham had put him in touch with Stephen Day, whose job was to deal with magical malpractice. Crane and Stephen had come very close to being murdered themselves before Stephen had ended the matter with a spectacular display of power. Five people had died that day, and since Crane had no idea if that was generally known or something Stephen wanted kept quiet, he simply added, "He was highly efficient."

Rackham snorted. "Efficient. Yes, you could say he's that."

"He saved my life on three occasions over the space of a week," Crane said. "I'd go so far as to call him competent."

"You like him, don't you?"

"Day? He's pleasant enough. Why?"

Rackham concentrated on straightening some papers against the corner of Crane's desk. "Well. You were with him at Sheng's last week."

"I was," Crane agreed. "Did you know I've taken a thirty percent share there? You must come with me again sometime. Tonight, unless you've a previous engagement?"

Rackham, who never turned down free meals, didn't respond to that. "What did Day make of Sheng's food?"

Crane repressed a grin at the memory of Stephen's first encounter with Szechuan pepper. "I think he was rather startled. It didn't stop him eating. I've never met anyone who eats so much."

"Have you had many meals with him?"

"I've bought him a couple of dinners as thanks. Is there a reason you ask? Because really, my dear fellow, if you're after any particular information, you know him better than I do."

"I know he's like you," Rackham said.

"Like me." Crane kept his tone easy. "Yes, the resemblance is striking. I could be looking in a mirror."

Rackham gave an automatic smile at that. Stephen Day had reddish brown curls to Crane's sleek and imperceptibly greying light blond, and pale skin to Crane's weather-beaten tan; he was twenty-nine years old to Crane's thirty-seven and appeared younger, and mostly, he stood a clear fifteen inches shorter than Crane's towering six foot three.

"I didn't mean you look like him," Rackham said unnecessarily. "I meant...you know. Your sort." He switched to Shanghainese to clarify. "Love of the silken sleeve. Oh, come off it, Vaudrey. I know he's a pansy."

"Really?" This wasn't a conversation Crane intended to have with Rackham or anyone else. Not in England, not where it was a matter of disgrace and long years in prison. "Are you asking me for my assessment of Day's tastes? Because I'd say they were none of my damned business or yours."

"You dined with him at Sheng's," repeated Rackham, with a sly look.

"I dine with lots of people at Sheng's. I took Leonora Hart there a couple of weeks ago, and I defy you to read anything into that. Come to that, I took *you* there and I don't recall you gave me more than a handshake."

Rackham flushed angrily. "Of course I didn't. I'm not your sort."

"Or my type." Crane let a mocking hint of lechery into his tone and saw Rackham's jaw tighten. "But even if you were, my dear chap, I can assure you I wouldn't tell your business to the world. Now, is there anything I can do for you?"

Rackham took a grip on himself. "I know you, Vaudrey. You can't play virtuous with me."

"I don't play virtuous with anyone. But since Stephen Day's love life is no concern of mine—"

"I don't believe you," said Rackham.

"Did you just call me a liar? Oh, don't even answer that. I'm busy, Rackham. I've got a sheaf of lading bills to reckon up and a factor to catch out. I assume you came here for something other than lubricious thoughts about mutual acquaintances. What do you want?"

Rackham looked away. His sandy hair was greying and his thin face was pouchy and worn, but the gesture reminded Crane of a sulky adolescent.

"I want you to make me a loan." He stared out of the window as he spoke.

"A loan. I see. What do you have in mind?"

"Five thousand pounds." Rackham's voice was defiant but he didn't look round.

Crane found himself momentarily speechless. "Five thousand pounds," he repeated at last.

"Yes."

"I see. Well, I'd be the first to admit that I owe you a favour, but—"

"You're good for it."

"Not in petty cash." The astronomical sum mentioned was ten years' income for a well-paid clerk. "What terms do you have in mind? What security would you offer?"

"I wasn't thinking of terms." Rackham turned, but his eyes merely skittered across Crane's face and away again. "I thought it would be an…open-ended agreement. Without interest."

Crane kept his features still and calm, but the nerves were firing along his skin, and he felt a cold clench in his gut at what was coming, as well as the first upswell of rage.

"You want me to give you five thousand pounds, which you propose not to pay back? Why would I do that, Rackham?"

Rackham met his eyes this time. "You owe me. I saved your life."

"The devil you did. You made an introduction."

"I introduced you to Day. You owe me for that."

"I don't owe you five thousand pounds for it."

"You owe it to me for keeping quiet about you and Day." Rackham's lips were rather pale and his skin looked clammy. "We're not in China now."

"Let's be clear. Are you trying to blackmail me?"

"That's such an ugly word," said Rackham predictably.

"Then it suits you, you pasty-faced junk-sick turd." Crane strode forward. He had a good six inches on Rackham, and although he was often described as lean, that was in large part an illusion caused by his height; people tended not to realise how broad-shouldered he was till he was uncomfortably close.

Rackham realised it now and took a step away. "Don't threaten me! You'll regret it!"

"I haven't threatened you, you worthless coward, nor will I. I'll just go straight to the part where I break your arms."

Rackham retreated another two steps and held up a hand. "I'll hurt you first. I'll ruin Day." He pointed a trembling finger. "Two years' hard labour. You might be able to buy your way out of trouble, perhaps, but he'll be finished. Disgraced. They'll dismiss him. I'll destroy him."

"With what, tales of a dinner at Sheng's? Go to hell."

"He goes to your rooms." Rackham moved to put a chair between himself and Crane. "At night. He came back with you after Sheng's and didn't leave till ten the next day, and—"

"You've been *spying* on me," Crane said incredulously. "You contemptible prick."

"Don't touch me! I can ruin him, and I will, if you lay a finger on me."

"The hell you will. You're terrified of him. That's why you've brought this horseshit to me. If you tried this on Stephen, he'd mince you into dog food, you hopeless fucking *flit*." Crane spat out the last word, the worst insult he knew to offer a practitioner, with all the contempt he could muster.

Colour rushed to Rackham's cheeks. For a second, Crane thought he would lash out, and braced himself, but Rackham kept control with a visible effort.

"I know what you're doing." His voice trembled with anger. "Well, it won't work. If you attack me, I'm allowed to defend myself. And I'm not going to touch you with power until then, whatever you call me. So your little boy friend can't touch me. Justiciars have to obey the law too, you know, and sodomy is a crime, so I can say what I want and he can't stop me, and if you want me to keep quiet, you'd better give me my money!"

"It's not your money. It's mine. And I'd rather spend all of it on lawyers than give you a penny. Now get out of my sight."

Rackham's eyes were wild. "I'll go to the Council. I'll report Day. I'll tell the police. They arrested that baronet just last month, they'll arrest you too. They won't care about your family name or your title."

"Nor do I," said Crane. "So I suggest you go practise your extortion on somebody who gives a monkey's balls for what you have to say. Get out. And give my regards to Merrick when you see him."

"Merrick?"

"Merrick. My manservant, remember?"

"Why would I see Merrick?" asked Rackham blankly.

"Well, perhaps you won't. But some night soon, in a dark alley, or near a nice deep ditch, or in the back room of some opium den, I expect he'll see you. In fact, I'm sure of it. Now fuck off, and shut the door behind you."

Rackham had gone a liverish colour, as well he might—Crane's henchman had been notorious in even the darkest back ways of Shanghai. He tried to say something; Crane hand-waved irritably and went back to his desk. After a few seconds Rackham managed, "You've got three days to change your mind. You give me my money by Friday, or I go to the Council and the police. And if I see Merrick, I'll, I'll…"

"You'll soil your trousers and beg for mercy." Crane picked up a bill and turned his attention to it. "But don't worry. I'll tell him to make sure you don't see him coming."

Rackham muttered something and stormed out. Crane waited a few seconds, heard the door slam, took a very deep breath.

He had never been blackmailed before. He *had* been expelled from three schools for gross immorality and thrown out of the country at the age of seventeen for his unlawful tastes, but that had been part of his war against his father, and he had fought it openly. And since then he had lived in China, where the laws of man and God were sublimely uninterested in who he shared his bed with. Eight months back in England hadn't instilled the constant sense of fear and persecution and terror of exposure that might have led him to bow to Rackham's demands.

He had considered the problem before he returned to England, of course, and had determined before his ship even reached Portsmouth that, if he ever faced arrest, he would bribe anyone necessary, post bail, and be on the next ship back to China. It would be effortless, he would feel no shame in running, and frankly, he would be glad to go home.

That had been before Stephen. Irresistible, astonishing, intriguing, fiercely independent Stephen, with his implacable sense of justice, and so very many enemies.

He could not, in conscience, run and leave Stephen alone. He had a responsibility there.

Crane frowned, considering how bad this might be. Stephen was wary and cautious, as most men's men were in this country, but he had said he wasn't at risk. He had said that he preferred, like any sensible man, to avoid trouble, but the Practitioners' Council turned a blind eye to nonmagical peccadilloes and eccentric private lives that hurt nobody. He had said he could use his powers to prevent any difficulty with mundane law.

Unfortunately, as Crane was well aware, Stephen was a fluent and unrepentant liar. He would have lied about danger to himself with no compunction, and Rackham clearly felt he had enough to serve as a serious threat.

Stephen needed to know about this, and quickly.

Crane scrawled a neutrally worded summons and put Stephen's address on it, a room in a small boarding house north of Aldgate. He had never set foot there himself, probably never would for fear of discovery, but he couldn't imagine a note would bring Stephen's life crashing down around his ears, and if it might, then that just made the Rackham situation all the more urgent. He had no other way to get in touch with his elusive lover, and so he put the whole business firmly to the back of his mind, locked up, and headed out to find a hansom and some distraction.

Merrick would be in Limehouse, most likely, and if he wasn't then Chinese friends would be, but Crane would have to trawl the pubs and gambling dens to track anyone down and, alone and too well dressed, that was not a risk he was prepared to take. Most of his English friends were school or social acquaintances and would doubtless be entertaining themselves at the sort of elegant evening event he abhorred, so, for the lack of anything better to do, he headed off for the Far Eastern Mercantile club, known as the Traders.

CHAPTER TWO

The Traders was frequented by travellers, businessmen, a smattering of explorers and scholars: anyone who had travelled further East than India and wanted to talk about it. It was not busy, but there was a small group of old China hands that he knew, so Crane joined them, pulling up a deep leather armchair to savour a very decent whisky and listen to "Town" Cryer's latest news.

Town, whose real first name Crane had long forgotten, finished an account of a piece of triple dealing involving Macau import-export law to a general murmur of approbation, and turned to Crane, who contributed an amusing anecdote about his purchase of a minority holding in Sheng's.

"Oh, jolly good, Vaudrey!" said Shaycott, a Java man. "Crane, I mean. You always tell a good story. You should come more often, we haven't seen you here in an age."

"I've been cursed busy with family matters." Crane acknowledged the sympathetic nods. "What news, Town? Bring me up to date."

"Well," said Town thoughtfully. "I suppose you heard about Merton?"

Crane twitched a lip with distaste. "What about him? Got on a boat, I hope?"

"His last voyage." Shaycott intoned the words. "Dead, just last week."

A youngish, tanned fellow, slightly the worse for drink, murmured, "Oh, dear, poor chap. I, er, should we…?" He started to raise his glass.

"I'm not drinking to Merton," said Humphris flatly. He was another Shanghai trader, one of the few Crane liked rather than tolerated through habit.

"I'll drink to his passing," Crane added. "Accident, or did an outraged parent catch up with him?"

"Accident, cleaning his gun." Town gave a meaningful cough.

"Not just a swine but a coward." Humphris spoke contemptuously, and then looked at Crane with sudden horror, no doubt recalling that his father and brother had both killed themselves. "Good God, Vaudrey, I'm terribly sorry. I didn't mean—"

"Not at all." Crane waved it away. "And in any case, I agree with you."

"Still, I beg your pardon." Humphris cast about for a change of subject. "Oh, have you heard about Willetts? You know, the copra dealer. Did you see in the papers?"

"No, what?"

"Murdered."

"Good God." Crane sat up. "Are you serious? Is there an arrest?"

"No, none. He was found in Poplar, by the river. Stabbed, apparently. A footpad."

"The devil. Poor fellow."

"Willetts and Merton, within a fortnight." Shaycott kept up the portentous tone.

"Yes, the subscription book here is going to start looking thin at this rate," Crane agreed heartlessly, and Town added, "The Curse of the Traders."

"Don't joke about that, you fellows. I've heard some things in my time—" Shaycott ignored the susurrus of irritation this kind of remark always produced, and launched into a tale. It was one of the deceased Willetts' stories, a lengthy yarn involving rats the size of dogs, but Crane had heard it several times before and found Shaycott dull even telling the best of tales. He drifted off into a reverie, wondering whether Stephen might be curled up in his bed when he returned home, and what he would do if he was. His attention was only recalled when Humphris waved a copy of *The Times* in his face.

"Look sharp, Vaudrey! I was asking if you've seen this? The Engagements column?"

"Oddly enough, I haven't read it today. Are we to wish you happy, Monk?"

"Monk" Humphris, who was as confirmed a bachelor as Crane, although in his case because of a natural inclination to celibacy, made a rude gesture. "Not me, you fool. Leonora Hart is getting married."

"The devil she is!"

"Oh, you hadn't heard?" said Town. "I had wind of it some time back. The chap's smitten, by all accounts."

Crane grabbed the newspaper and scrutinised it. "Eadweard Blaydon? How do you even *say* that?"

"It's pronounced Edward. Politician. Member of Parliament. He's a reformer. Rooting out corruption. End the sale of honours and the benefits of clergy and the pernicious practices of bribery. An honest mandarin."

There was a dubious murmur at that. Most of those present regarded bribery as something between a handy tool and a form of tax; none of them had high opinions of mandarins of any nationality.

"Do you think she's told him about Hart?" an unpopular man named Peyton remarked snidely. "If there was an official in Shanghai he didn't bribe, I never met him."

"Hart was no fool," Crane said. "Blaydon will have a job on his hands to match up."

"Is that why Mrs. Hart hasn't remarried? Hart's glorious memory?" Peyton's voice was sneering. "Because *I* heard there was some sort of scandal with some Singapore man. Town, do *you* know—"

"Tom and Leonora Hart were two of the best friends I've ever had," Crane interrupted, locking eyes with Peyton. "Hart saved my skin more than once. His death devastated Leo. If she is able to marry again, I'm damned glad for her, and if any of you feel the urge to spread spiteful fishwives' gossip about her or Tom, I suggest you resist it." Peyton went red. "Leo is perfectly capable of defending her own honour," Crane went on, loudly enough that the other conversations in the room were suspended, "and I'm sure Blaydon can and will do so for her as well, but just to be clear, I will take any offensive comments about Leonora Hart as a direct personal affront, and I *will* make the speaker eat his words, at the end of my boot if need be."

"I'll back you up on that," Monk Humphris said.

"Sir, I don't like your tone to my uncle." The young man stood as he spoke, slightly too violently.

"And I don't like your uncle's tone, so it evens out," Crane replied, and stood too, staring down at the young man for a couple of deliberately intimidating seconds, before going over to pour himself another whisky from the tantalus. This allowed Monk and the others time to persuade the young man to sit down and be quiet. The words "disgraceful" and "lawless" were audible in Peyton's nasal voice; "quite right", "bad man to cross" and "that vicious brute Merrick" came from the others. Judging that a sufficiently comprehensive analysis of his capabilities to put the young spark off, Crane strolled back to his chair, deciding that he'd find out what the hell Leo was playing at in the morning.

Stephen lay naked, arms spread wide, the Magpie Lord's ring glowing on his finger, illuminating the fingers that curled like claws.

He writhed and twisted, uttering incoherent pleas for mercy as his silky cock jutted hard from the reddish curls at his groin.

"Please, my lord, please," he was sobbing, as Crane positioned himself at the entrance to the small sinewy body.

"Please what?" Crane demanded, nudging the tip of his cock against Stephen's arse. "Please *what*?"

Stephen howled, arching his back, thrusting himself towards Crane. "Please, my lord!"

Crane pushed his shoulders down hard. "One more chance, pretty boy."

"Make me yours. Make me fly. Make the magpies fly."

"You will fly." Now he was thrusting in the dark heat of Stephen's body, watching the birds flutter on his lover's skin, the black and white flicker over his amber eyes. The seven tattoos silently shrieked and flapped, and magpies were rising all around them in a storm of wings and cawing as feathers spread wide from Stephen's extended arms. "*Fly*," Crane said again, and came hard and hot as the magpies screamed.

He woke up thrashing in a tangle of sheets and an empty bed, sweating, bewildered, and with an unmistakeable sticky wetness on his belly.

"Fuck," he muttered aloud and let his head drop back onto the hot pillow as he tried to shake off the dream.

It had only been a few days, damn it. Nocturnal emissions seemed hardly appropriate at his advanced age. And he was beginning to lose patience with the bloody magpies.

Crane, though without magical talent of his own, was the last descendant of the Magpie Lord, a hugely powerful sorcerer, and in some way he didn't understand he—his blood, his body—acted as a conduit between his ancestor's power and Stephen's talent. One of the more bizarre side effects of this was that Crane's seven tattoos of magpies took on independent life when he and Stephen fucked, flying and hopping across both men's skin. One had decided it preferred Stephen and had taken up permanent residence on his back, leaving Crane with the frankly unsettling experience of looking in a mirror and seeing plain unmarked skin where a tattoo used to be, and Stephen the equally disturbing gift of a tattoo that he'd never had inked. Crane could live without the damned birds invading his imaginary love life as well.

He touched a hand to his shoulder, where the defecting tattoo had once spread its wings, uttered a curse on magpies, dreams and absent lovers, shifted into a less sticky patch of sheet, and went back to sleep.

CHAPTER THREE

The next day, there was no word from Stephen by eleven, which was when Crane called on Leonora Hart.

Leo Callas had been a coltish fifteen-year-old when he'd first met her, nearly two decades ago. Her father had been a trader, her mother long dead. She had run wild in the Shanghai streets, trading halls and merchant palaces all her life, and could curse in English, Spanish, and Shanghainese with as much fluency as any of the young men around her. At seventeen she had abruptly blossomed into beauty and, armed with her father's fat purse, had been set to go to London and become a Success. Instead, to everyone's astonishment except Lucien Vaudrey's, she had at eighteen eloped with Tom Hart, a silk trader of forty-two years, dubious reputation, and no appeal at all to her father.

Lucien Vaudrey had been unsurprised because she had confided her elopement plans to him, and in fact he and Merrick had taken on the slightly unconventional groomsmen roles of overpowering the gatekeepers at the Callas compound to let Leo out that night.

He had played his part without hesitation, because Tom had been kind to him in a life that had been very bare of kindness, and because he was twenty-two and didn't expect to last to twenty-three. By the time he was old enough that he might have regretted his role in such an obviously disastrous match, it had become clear that Tom and Leonora were two halves of a soul.

Tom Hart had died some eight years ago, of a heart attack. Leonora had been almost deranged with grief, starving herself, drinking too much, acting in a way that shocked even the least shockable.

There was no trace of that wild, crazed widow now, any more than of the tomboyish girl. Leonora Hart was a very lovely woman at thirty-four. She was tall and curvaceous, with rich black hair and striking brown eyes, high cheekbones, and skin dark enough to seem exotic without raising too many prurient whispers about mixed parentage. Today she wore silk in a shade of dull orange that was a perfect foil for her autumnal eyes, and looked beautiful, elegant, sophisticated, and wildly out of place in the conventionally overdecorated drawing room of her aunt's house, where she had been staying for the last two months.

"Leo, darling, you look magnificent," said Crane, sweeping her hand to his lips.

She pulled him into a hug. "You rotten aristo. First you become a peer, now you're playing the gentleman. What's next, Lady Crane and some chicks?"

"Good God, don't say such things. Anyway, isn't it you who's nesting? Why did I not know about this?"

"Oh sweet heaven." Leonora rolled her eyes. "I suppose you've seen *The Times*. I could have *shaken* Eadweard."

"But you are engaged?"

"Yes. Well—we are, but it wasn't supposed to come out yet."

"Why on earth not?"

Leonora gestured to a pair of chairs and sat. She leaned in to him, and he mimicked her, knowing that the English cousins with whom she lived were far too respectable for her liking. He wasn't surprised when she spoke in Shanghainese.

"I like Eadweard very much. I want to marry him. I really do. Only..." Leonora knitted her fingers together. "You understand why I married Jan Ahl, don't you?"

"Because it was the anniversary of Tom's death, and you'd been drunk for the best part of a week, and in bed with Ahl for much of that, and marrying him was one alternative to killing yourself, although not the best one."

"I love you for your kindness, Lucien," Leonora said wryly. "But you do understand. Because you knew Tom, and you knew what we had, and you know how I grew up, and how things are back home. It's not like that here."

"That it isn't."

"And Eadweard's not like Tom," Leonora went on. "I don't suppose I could love him if he was. He's—he's righteous. Do you know what I mean? He doesn't lie. He has high standards and lives by them. He would never let me down, never do a dishonest thing."

"You're right. He's not like Tom."

"No." She grinned reminiscently. "Tom was the most lawless man I ever knew. He always said he never let a friend down—"

"But sometimes people didn't know they weren't friends any more until it was too late."

"Hah! Yes. And, I loved Tom, but I'm older now and I've been alone for so long and...Eadweard's a truly good man, and I respect that. I don't suppose you know what I mean about righteousness, but—"

"An honesty that's basically untouchable. Someone who will break before he bows. There's a sort of purity to it. Yes, I know the appeal."

"Well," Leonora said. "That's the problem."

"Blaydon does know about Hart, doesn't he?"

"Of course. That is, I haven't gone into too much detail. He thinks Tom was a scoundrel just for eloping with me, so I certainly wouldn't tell him about his business dealings."

"And what does he think about Ahl?"

"I haven't told him."

Crane digested that for a moment. "You haven't told your fiancé about your second husband."

"No."

"You have told him you *had* a second husband?"

"No."

"Because…"

"Because I slept with Ahl before we married, and I married him while I was drunk, and when he hit me, I had him beaten half to death and thrown on a ship to nowhere, and then I divorced him in his absence. And every single part of that would revolt Eadweard, and even if I didn't tell him any of it…" She took a deep breath. "He doesn't approve of divorce. Not even for the best reasons, conducted in the best way."

Crane wasn't entirely convinced that Leonora's divorce was legal at all, done as it had been by a few words from a friendly and inebriated magistrate. "Leo, are you sure this engagement is a good idea?"

"Yes. He doesn't have to know. It was a mistake, it's done with."

"All right. So why are you worried about the announcement in the papers? Either Ahl is out of your life or he's not. You haven't heard from him, have you?"

"No, no." Leonora sounded dismissive, but there was a thin line of worry between her brows. "No. He's not the trouble."

"So what is?"

She looked away, and the truth dawned on Crane like the morning of an execution.

"Leo, have you by any chance had a visit from Theodore Rackham recently?"

She spun back to face him. "How did you— Oh God, not you too?"

"He came to see me yesterday."

"Oh, damn him. The little shit." Leonora bit her lip, worry in her eyes. "You have to be careful, Lucien, this ridiculous country will put you in prison without a thought. What are you going to do? Have you paid him?"

"Have I hell. I told him to fuck off. I always said I'd leave this damned island in a heartbeat rather than submit to blackmail. And I would…"

Leonora looked narrowly at him. "But?"

Crane sighed. "But someone else is involved."

"Your righteous man?"

"I beg your pardon?"

"Oh, please, Lucien, I do listen to you." The conspiratorial grin he knew so well lit up her face. "Go on, tell me. Who is he? Can I meet him? Is he handsome? How long has this been going on? He's not married, is he? Are you in love?"

"Calm down, woman," said Crane, laughing. "Er…that's hard to explain, no, not precisely handsome but very appealing, about four months, not married, and…I enjoy his company. I'd call him a just man, rather than a righteous one, though."

"Interesting distinction. Does Merrick like him?"

"Very much. Likes him, respects him, and is just a little bit afraid of him."

"*Really.*" Leonora sat up straight. "What kind of man frightens Merrick?"

"A just one, of course. You'd like him, Leo. Rackham, however, doesn't, and has threatened to destroy him unless I pay up."

That quenched the brief spurt of laughter in Leonora's eyes. "Can he?"

"Possibly. I need to talk to him. My lover, not Rackham. So what's he threatening you with?"

"He said he'd tell Eadweard everything. About Ahl and that week before I married him. He said he'll tell Eadweard I'm not divorced, and you know, it will be dreadfully hard to prove I am, and even if I do… Eadweard doesn't believe in it, he thinks that what God has joined, men should not put asunder. I know he loves me, but I think he'll leave me if he finds out all this."

"You could just deny it."

"I could try, but…well, if he started looking… It would destroy everything. He wouldn't trust me again." Her eyes were wide with hurt at the thought.

"No, probably not." Crane felt a momentary sympathy for the absent Blaydon. "You know, the proper course at this point would be to confess everything. Either Blaydon will forgive it all and you're happy forever, or he won't but you'll both know where you stand."

"No." Her voice was flat. "I shan't. I don't see that I deserve to have my chance at a new life spoiled by something that, honestly, thousands of other people do every day. Why should I live as a nun because I made a mistake seven years ago? How often did you get drunk and wake up in someone's bed? What about that warlord?"

"Don't remind me. I'm not arguing, but I'm not Blaydon either. And it won't be any better if he finds out after you're married."

"That's why I wanted to wait," Leonora said. "But Eadweard doesn't want to. He wants children. I've told him I never could with Tom but he's willing to take the chance."

"Good for him. What exactly were you hoping this wait would achieve? How is this going to go away?"

She gave a little helpless shrug. "I don't *know*. I don't know what to do."

"How much have you paid Rackham?"

"Three hundred pounds, last week. He wants more. He sent a note this morning saying he'd call tomorrow. He must have seen that damned notice."

"Hmm." Crane frowned. "He asked me for five thousand."

"*How* much?"

"And…Merton's dead, did you hear? Last week."

"Good."

"Yes, Leo, but he killed himself. And if anyone was susceptible to blackmail it would be him."

"Oh," Leonora said slowly. "So…Rackham killed the goose that laid the golden egg, and now he's looking for more geese?"

"Or, he needs a lot of money fast. He's given me till Friday to come up with the five thousand."

"Someone's on his back. Gambling debts? Opium debts?"

"My thoughts exactly."

Leonora's dark eyes met his. "Can you find out who he owes?"

"I'm getting Merrick onto it this afternoon."

"What are you thinking of?"

"Offering him passage on a boat and a fat purse. If he's under the cosh, he might jump at a chance to get away."

Leonora looked dubious. "What if it's the kind of people you can't escape?"

"We'll find out. Don't worry. Stall him if you can, pay him if you can't. I'll have him dealt with one way or the other in the next two days."

"And…what about the other way?" asked Leonora.

There was a short silence. Crane said, "I don't know."

"I know what Tom would have done."

"So do I. And I've considered it. I even told him I'd send Merrick after him. But I don't think I could explain to—my just man—that I'd set up a murder, Leo. I don't think I'd want to try."

"Is it murder to kill a blackmailer?"

"Maybe not," Crane said. "Not if you're desperate. I'm not desperate yet."

CHAPTER FOUR

The rest of the day was intensely tiresome. Crane put Merrick abreast of the situation and sent him off to snout out Rackham's woes among his many Chinese drinking and gambling friends. He contacted his bankers to make sure he had enough cash in hand to bail himself, Stephen and Merrick out of whatever the law might throw at them and get them all urgently out of the country, then he thought about it again and increased the sum so that he could get Leonora out too if need be. It probably wouldn't be necessary, but one never knew.

He looked over his affairs to ensure that he had covered the most immediate issues if he had to cut and run. He responded curtly to various letters from a cousin several times removed, making demands on him in his unacknowledged and unwanted capacity as head of the house. He had an irritatingly frank discussion with his lawyer as to what to do in the case of arrest on charges of unnatural acts. Mostly, he resisted, with increasing difficulty, the urge to go round to Stephen's rooms, or to send more and more messages. Stephen would reappear when it suited him.

He ate alone at a chop house since Merrick was still out, and was stretched out on the couch reading the latest number of *All the Year Round* with limited interest when he heard the door open.

"About bloody time," he called, without looking up, as soft feet approached. "Well?"

There was no reply. But Crane felt a pressure on his waist, and glanced down to see his top button silently undoing itself, slipping through the buttonhole apparently of its own accord.

"Hello, Stephen," he said, without looking round.

"Hello," said Stephen, and dropped to his knees by the couch as the remaining buttons flicked open one by one.

Blood, bone and birdspit, Stephen called it: a deep-rooted, old and strange type of magic that could tap the massive power inherent to Crane's bloodline. The affair in spring had been an attempt by a group of warlocks to claim the Magpie Lord's magic using the abused corpses of the Vaudrey family. Stephen had wrested the power back when he had shared Crane's blood. The third item on the list, birdspit, was a country euphemism, and a much less effective route to the power, but then, power wasn't the point of the exercise.

Stephen's mouth was hot and eager on Crane's cock now, sliding up and down the shaft, tongue flickering round the smooth head. His hands, those magical hands that prickled with power, were on Crane's thighs and hips, stroking the magpie tattoos that adorned him, the tingling of his fingers getting stronger as Stephen's own arousal built, feeding off Crane's unconcealed pleasure. He was apparently intent on bringing Crane off with mouth alone, tongue playing up and down the long vein, lips tightening with wicked force, teeth nipping just to the right side of painful, then pulling his mouth off and down to lavish attention on his balls again. Crane gave a groan of agony at the withdrawal and glanced at Stephen's russet head, catching him shooting a mischievous look up.

Well, that could not stand. Crane took a handful of curly hair and pulled, not gently. "You. Get your mouth back on my cock. Now."

Stephen's hands gave a flare of arousal that stabbed into Crane's hipbones like needles of light as he obediently took Crane back into his mouth and sucked hard, mouth working with a tight clutch.

"Good boy," Crane said. "Now get hold of yourself. I want you coming with my prick down your throat. And don't you dare take your mouth off me."

Stephen whimpered through his mouthful as he slipped a hand to his own groin and began to work himself frantically as he sucked. His other hand gripped Crane's thigh, the power surging through them starting to take on the staccato pulsing beat that Crane knew well.

"Christ, you love that, don't you?" he said roughly. "On your knees with a prick in your mouth and another in your hand. Frig yourself harder. Harder."

Stephen's rhythm stumbled. He pulled slightly back and said indistinctly around Crane's erection, "I'll fuck my hand if you fuck my mouth."

Crane's balls tightened almost painfully at that: dirty talk for Stephen was a matter of desperation, of the best possible kind.

"Witch." He gripped the little man's hair more tightly and pulled him forward. "And don't talk with your mouth full."

He took charge then, rocking his hips, thrusting as deep as he dared. Stephen's hand on his leg was pulsing violently with pleasure at the rough usage as he attempted to keep control of his lips and tongue; then he made an agonised, urgent noise in his throat, his body jerking, the orgasm spangling through his fingers like shards of glass; and Crane let go all restraint and thrust without mercy, feeling Stephen's strangled cries vibrating over his cock as he came hard, spilling into the back of his lover's mouth.

Stephen choked for a second, gagged slightly, then swallowed, as Crane flopped bonelessly back on the couch, letting the aftershocks of pleasure ebb away before propping himself up on his elbows to take a look at his lover.

The smaller man was sitting on his heels, licking his lips. He had lines of tiredness round his eyes, and there were a couple of nasty scratches on his face. He was scruffier than usual, in that he looked as if he'd slept in his cheap suit, or more accurately, as if he had failed to sleep in it. But his tawny eyes had the golden glow that fucking and sucking always gave him, the combination of pleasure and borrowed power, and that foxy smile was twitching at the edge of his agile mouth.

Crane reached out and pulled him over for a kiss.

"Apart from that," he said, "have you eaten?"

They sat in the kitchen, at the plain wooden table, while Stephen worked his way through a slab of cold chicken pie and Crane kept him company with a glass of wine and a story he didn't want to tell.

Stephen listened in silence to Rackham's threats. They didn't spoil his appetite, but the sparkle went from his eyes, and Crane looked at the lines of exhaustion on his face and felt loathing of Rackham harden in his gut.

"Interesting," Stephen said at last. "He came to you, not me."

"You don't have any money."

"No, true, but... He's made himself noticed by the justiciary recently. I'd have thought he might have asked me for an easier ride."

"And what would you have done if he attempted to blackmail you into dereliction of duty? He's not a complete idiot, he must know how well you'd take that."

"Whereas you just gave him five thousand pounds?" enquired Stephen.

"No, but I'm ready to give him something. Money and passage home."

"Really?" Stephen put his fork down. "Lucien—"

"We're not alone in this," Crane said. "He's also threatening a friend of mine. And a third man killed himself just last week. He might well have been another victim."

"Was he a friend too?" asked Stephen with quick concern.

"No, a loathsome piece of work, he was no loss. I'm guessing about him, of course, but it seems too much coincidence that another

Shanghai man should have chosen this week to kill himself. I was of the opinion that Rackham needed cash urgently to pay someone off— that's where Merrick is, trying to find out who—but if he's on the wrong side of your lot, perhaps he's just gathering funds to make a run for it. Either way, I'm prepared to pay him to leave the country."

Stephen chewed his last mouthful of pie, frowning a little. "He's not in that much trouble with us. So perhaps he's up to something I don't know about yet."

"Talking of trouble," Crane said. "How bad is this for you? Honestly, please."

Stephen propped his elbows on the table and ran the end of the fork over his thumb. "Well. The justiciary have no obligation to investigate normal, unskilled crimes, as such." He tapped the points of the fork thoughtfully. The metal tines peeled apart, like flower petals. "If Rackham reports me to the Council or the justiciary for vice, it would be quite awful and humiliating, but no more than that. There aren't enough justiciars for them to discard any lightly." He ran a finger along one of the tines and watched it spiral. "But abusing one's powers to cover up one's crimes of any kind is a different matter. If I came to the attention of the police for, you know, what we do—well, I've always intended to deal with that situation by, er…" He waved the fork vaguely.

"Abusing your powers?"

"In a controlled way."

"Naturally," said Crane dryly. "But is there any reason you couldn't do that now? Would Rackham be able to tell, or prove, you'd done that?"

Stephen didn't answer immediately. His attention was apparently fixed on the other three tines of the fork, which were weaving themselves into a plait.

Crane, who hadn't got rich by jumping in to fill silences, waited.

"If I was on a watch list, it would be difficult," Stephen said at last. "That is, if one is suspected of warlockry, or abusing one's powers, one's partner and colleagues can be tasked to keep an eye out, and to come down hard at any sign of impropriety. When you're on a watch list, you're a marked man, and there is no benefit of the doubt. If I was on a watch list, and I had a run-in with the police, I could be in a lot of trouble if I used my powers. And if I *didn't* use them, I'd be in a lot of trouble too, because I'd be arrested. So, yes, that would be bad."

"And Rackham could get you put on a watch list?"

Stephen wrapped the thin metal handle slowly round his finger, as if it were paper. "No. No, he couldn't do that. Not at all. I've spoiled your fork."

"I have more."

"Rich in forks." Stephen dropped the coiled metal onto the table. "Let's talk about this later, Lucien. I want to go to bed."

It should have been a loving night, especially with the frustration of separation burned off. Crane felt a vulnerability in Stephen that filled his own body with a strange pain, and he made love accordingly, carefully and cherishingly. Stephen burrowed into him and he stroked the nape of the smaller man's neck as he kissed his ear, lavishing attention on the sensitive lobe till Stephen's breath was ragged. He kissed and stroked and licked his way along Stephen's body, holding him tight, then moved down to gently take his balls into his mouth, rolling them lightly with his tongue till his lover moaned, sliding an oiled finger into Stephen's arse and pressing with care, to arouse and not to tantalise. Stephen was warm and yielding and pliant tonight, and Crane felt a rush of tenderness as he watched the other man's face, eyes shut, head tilted back.

"It's all right, sweet boy, sweetheart," he murmured, moving to kneel between Stephen's legs. "I'll take care of you."

Stephen's eyes opened, and he met Crane's look with a wide amber gaze for a second. His expression was unreadable; it looked almost bleak. Then he shook his head, drew up his legs and rolled over to a kneeling position, facing away.

"Stephen?"

"Like this," Stephen said, his voice a little muffled.

"I can't kiss you like that." There was no position on earth that would let them kiss when they fucked. Crane didn't want to say that he wouldn't see distress on Stephen's face, or read his pleasure, or the lack of it, through the prickling of his hands. "Stephen, are you sure—"

"This, Lucien. Hard. I need this. Please."

Crane opened his mouth to protest, and stopped himself. Stephen had a taste for submission, of course, but on occasion he also used his body to quiet his mind, letting intense physical sensation block out sensitivities to things Crane couldn't see and memories he was glad not to share. At those times Stephen had a craving for rough treatment that Crane found slightly alarming, mostly because he was so much larger and stronger that he feared causing real hurt, and just a little because he was manhandling someone who could kill with a thought.

But Stephen knew what he wanted. Crane was disappointed, even irrationally angry that his lover's needs were so unusually out of kilter with his own desires. But it was obvious that the last few days had taken their toll, Stephen had made himself clear, and mostly, Crane couldn't make him take loving if he needed fucking.

"You want it like this?"

"*Yes*," said Stephen through his teeth.

"You asked for it."

He grabbed the smaller man, and pushed into his body, slowly but without stopping, making Stephen take his entire length in one long stroke. Stephen cried out with desperation and relief, and Crane fucked him punishingly hard, ruthlessly imposing his size and strength with every stroke till Stephen wailed aloud. He could hear the heavy gold ring Stephen wore on a chain round his neck thumping against his chest as it swung with each impact. Crane held him down throughout, gripping his narrow shoulders and pushing them into the bed, and soon enough the younger man came, in shivering spurts and with a sound like a sob, as the magpie tattoo fluttered frantically on his back.

Afterwards Stephen lay facing away. Crane curled an arm over his shoulder, brushing a finger softly over his sparse chest hair, and they lay body to body for a while in silence, as the tension drained out of Stephen and his knotted muscles relaxed.

Finally Crane said, "Will you tell me?"

A few moments passed before Stephen answered. "You asked if Rackham could get me on a watch list."

"And you said he couldn't. I take it that wasn't true."

"He doesn't have to. I'm already on one."

Crane's hand stilled. "A watch list names suspected warlocks. You are suspected."

"Yes."

"Since when?"

"A few weeks. I found out two days ago."

"*Why*?"

Stephen shook his head. "Doesn't matter."

"Yes it does! You, a warlock? I've never heard such bollocks. You! Are they bloody mad?"

Stephen reached for Crane's hand. The electric prickle of his touch wrapped warmly round Crane's slender fingers. "Thank you, Lucien. It's nice to have a defender."

"What about your partner? Why isn't she defending you?"

Stephen's fingers twitched. "Because she's watching me."

"The bitch!"

"It's not her fault," Stephen snapped. "She wasn't even supposed to tell me. She's had orders, she can't ignore it."

"Ignore *what*? Why would anyone think that?"

"Oh, it's stupid. It's mostly a misunderstanding, really. It's you."

"Me?"

Stephen sighed. "Lucien, every time we, you know, do anything, it leaves me flying. You, in me, the Magpie Lord, the power. I can't hide it. People *notice*. I've got a source of external power and nobody knows what it is and…"

He tailed off. Crane waited, unsure of his meaning, and then abruptly realized what he didn't want to say.

"Are you telling me your colleagues think you're stripping people?" He had seen first-hand the effects of that practice, when warlocks used other people as sources of power and drained the life from them in the process. Stephen had told him that particular exploitation was what defined a warlock. "But for God's sake, you wouldn't do that. Surely they know you wouldn't."

Stephen winced. "There's nothing else obvious to explain the power. *I* don't have an explanation. What are they supposed to think?"

"Can't you just tell them the truth?" Crane thought about that for two seconds and added, "Your partner, at least. Without going into detail."

"I could tell Esther what happens when you take me to bed, yes," Stephen said. "I really don't want to. Or I could simply explain that you are an immense source of power and hope she doesn't ask how I get at it, although of course she would. But yes, either way, I could tell her you're the source, and then she could take it back to the Council to explain why I shouldn't be on a watch list."

"Right. And you're not doing this because…?"

Stephen twisted round to face him. "Have you forgotten what happened the last time practitioners knew about the power in your blood?"

"They were warlocks."

"They were practitioners. You're a human source like none other, and you know how desperate we can get. You've seen it. The hunger for power makes the drive for money or sex look like a, a *hobby*, and you're a walking fountain of it. Don't you see? It would be like telling a pack of hungry dogs about a particularly juicy bone." He gave a half-laugh. "For God's sake. If word got round about what happens when we go to bed, there'd be a queue all down the street for your services. You'd have half the Council ready to bend over for you."

"How good-looking are your Council?"

"Not."

"Damn."

"It's the least of your worries," Stephen said. "Because the other half would already be thinking of how to get their hands on your blood, without consideration of your preferences."

"This is your Council you're talking about. They must be reputable people, surely?"

"Oh, it would all be reputable. There would be a 'need for study'. A 'consideration of the Magpie Lord's legacy'. An 'assessment of the greater good'. But it would mean they'd get their hands on you and not let go. Maybe they might let me see you—"

"*Let?*"

"I do not trust my colleagues in this matter." Stephen's voice was thin. "That's the size of it, Lucien. I think that too many people would want a piece of you, for what they could do through you, and I couldn't protect you from the best of them, let alone the worst."

Crane ran his fingers through Stephen's hair. "But would this bloody magpie business have to get out? Couldn't your partner explain for you without discussing the specifics?"

"Perhaps. I don't know. It would be a lot to put on her. It would be her duty to pass it on the Council, of course, but she makes her own judgements. She might cover for me if I told her everything. It's just…" A long pause. "I don't want to do that."

"I thought you trusted her."

"I do," Stephen said. "We trust each other with our lives. Literally. If I were to tell anyone, it would be her. But she still has me on a watch list, because she has to accept that I might turn. And I still don't want to tell her, because it's safer if nobody knows but me." His lips curved into something the same shape as a smile. "One can't be sentimental about practitioners, you see. Anyone can fall."

Crane shut his eyes against the misery in Stephen's face. "I don't want you sacrificing yourself to protect me. I'm not subject to your bloody Council."

"Let's keep it that way. And I'm not sacrificing myself. I'm not abusing my powers, I'm not a warlock, and I won't be caught, because I'm not doing anything wrong. This watch-list business is a misunderstanding, nothing more. It's just that it limits my options if I should run into trouble. That's all I'm worried about."

It clearly wasn't all. Crane sighed. "I can't stop you from being arrested, I suppose, but if you are, you do know that I will apply the entire resources of my wealth to dealing with it. Including the services of a firm of lawyers who are more like moray eels than human beings."

"Yes."

Crane frowned at the flat tone. "Stephen, I mean it. I won't let you go to trial, let alone prison. I can prevent that and I will."

"I know." Stephen wasn't looking at him.

"I'll give my lawyers your name," Crane went on. "They're entirely discreet. Then you can use them at will, without going through me."

"Though still dependent on you."

"Welcome to life for everyone else," Crane snapped, somewhat offended by the unappreciative response. "At least I've got money. There are plenty of people with neither money nor power who have to deal with this shit, so—"

"I know. Sorry. Thank you."

"I don't want your thanks. Just stop trying to stand alone when you don't have to. Accept some damned help, now and again. The rest of us do."

Stephen smiled tiredly at him and curled up under his arm, into his chest, but he didn't reply, and within a few moments, he was asleep.

CHAPTER FIVE

Crane woke the next morning to the sound of Merrick bringing him a cup of coffee. He opened an eye and registered that there was only one cup on the tray at the same time as he became conscious of the empty bed around him. He muttered a curse.

"Problem?" enquired his henchman.

"No. Nothing."

"Mr. Day didn't turn up, then?" said Merrick, homing in on his thoughts as ever.

"Been and gone."

"Came and went?"

"Oh, shut up." Crane sat up and sipped his coffee. God knew when Stephen had left, he hadn't even stirred, but the little sod had ways of moving around silently. There would, he knew, be no note. There never was.

And that was perfectly reasonable, because they were both free men who could do as they pleased. He would rather have found Stephen's small form curled under his arm, would definitely rather be having a slow, leisurely morning in bed with him, watching the laughter and the lust warm his tawny eyes to gold, but doubtless he was busy. Crane had learned not even to ask about his work, counting it only as "busy" or "not busy".

They really had needed to talk more about bloody Rackham. That was the only problem. Otherwise Stephen could come and go—thank you, Merrick—as he pleased, and it was absurd of Crane to feel hurt, let alone this sliver of fear that this time he wouldn't come back, that the whole damned magpie business and Rackham's blackmail might make Stephen decide that life would be safer lived alone.

Rackham. Crane's eyes narrowed as he watched Merrick move round the room. "Any luck yesterday?"

"Not a dicky bird." Merrick picked up a discarded sock. "No gambling, no junk debts. Nothing nobody's talking about. If Mr. Rackham's got himself in trouble, I reckon it's a shaman thing."

"He has got himself in shaman trouble," Crane said. "Stephen mentioned that, but he didn't think it was enough to warrant making a run for it. So he concluded Rackham must be up to something he doesn't know about."

"Suspicious-minded bugger, Mr. Day. So what about Mr. Rackham, then? Am I going to break his legs?"

"Not yet, no." Crane drained his cup. "He's battened onto Leonora Hart."

"The hell he has." Merrick's face darkened. "Why don't I break his fucking neck and have done?"

"Give it time. We've till Friday, he said. And we must act in a civilised fashion in this country, you know."

"If you say so, my lord," muttered Merrick. "What's Mr. Day think?"

"Says he should be fine. Says it isn't likely to be a problem."

"Believe him?"

"No. Come with me to the office today, I want you in Limehouse. I'm going to call in some obligations and do a bit more work on Rackham's affairs. Buy up some debts. Revive some old grudges. See how fast I can get him to the verge of ruin."

"Ah," said Merrick, satisfied. "*That* kind of civilised."

It was four o'clock when the summons came.

"My lord?" His clerk opened the office door with a perfunctory knock. "A message for you. Personal."

It was a girl, and not a very striking girl, at that. She had pinched features, with a sharp nose, dirty-blonde hair in a straggly chignon, a general air of scruffiness. Her face was grubby, but the dirt was superficial, not ground in; she evidently washed regularly, and her boots were reasonably new and sturdy. She looked about fifteen, for all that meant with city youths. She was flushed from running and had a paper gripped in her hand.

"You his la-a-awdship?" she drawled.

"I'm Lord Crane."

"Ooh." Her eyes widened with mock awe. They were a striking light silver-blue. "Well, Lord Crane, I got a message for you." She held out the paper.

It was a playbill, and the message was scrawled on the back in pencil.

My lord

If convenient, please accompany the bearer. Your help would be most welcome on a professional matter.

S. Day

Crane contemplated that for a second, keeping his face blank. It was beyond extraordinary that Stephen should be asking for help with his work, but it resembled what little Crane had seen of his hand, it was definitely a reference to their conversation the night before, and the salutation...

"My lord" in Stephen's voice wasn't a respectful address. The son of a solicitor, he had a great deal of the clerkly class's pride and fiercely refused to use terms that implied aristocratic superiority. He had never once used it to Crane, until they became lovers, and the game began. In bed (over a desk, against a wall), "my lord" was a breathless, frantic submission, a plea to be mastered, a wholehearted surrender to Crane's demands and desires. On the page, it made this letter as much a *billet-doux* as a summons, and thinking of Stephen writing the words gave Crane a jolt straight to the groin. Whatever the little sod was up to, he had known this would bring Crane running.

"I'll be with you in a moment," he said. "Merrick!"

Crane knew Limehouse reasonably well, but after following the girl through alleys and back ways for ten minutes, he was lost. Not utterly lost—he knew which way the river was and which way Ratcliffe Highway—but lost enough that he wouldn't have wanted to run for it. They were in the poorest parts of London now, where the faces on the street were filthy, slurred by alcohol, marked by disease, raw with hunger. There were a lot of Chinese, lascars, sailors. Every head turned to watch Crane's progress, his height and the perfectly tailored clothing and spotless shirt marking him out as a rich man, a potential victim, a pigeon worth plucking.

He had left Merrick at the office with several other jobs to do. The deeper they went into this no man's land, the more he had to resist fruitless regrets on that decision.

The girl turned down another dingy alley, so narrow the sun's rays would barely penetrate it at midday, and two men fell into step behind Crane. He turned, judged intent at a glance, and rapped out a string of hair-raising abuse to discourage any attempts on his life or purse.

"What you on about?" demanded the girl. "Come on."

"I don't much want to be coshed or have my throat slit." Crane glared at the two men.

"Yeah, never worry. I'll look after you. This way."

She swung into a dark, low doorway. Crane gave the two men a last, nasty look, and ducked under the lintel into close, hot darkness, following the vague shape of the girl's skirt round a couple more passages until he came out into a larger room.

It was windowless, lit by a few candles in lanterns. The floor was bare, and the walls sweated moisture. It smelled of cooking garlic and acrid chilli seeds, offal and sewers.

In the room were seven people. Four of them were Chinese, faces guarded, squatting against the far wall, waiting. The other three were European. One was a burly young man of medium height, with light brown hair, vivid green eyes and a square jaw. He stood against the wall with his arms folded, next to a large bundle of sackcloth. The next was a woman, aged perhaps thirty. She was plainly dressed, with dark hair twisted in a neat chignon, an olive-skinned face that was strong rather than attractive, and large, intensely brown eyes.

The last person in the room was Stephen. He was perched on the edge of a rickety table, amber eyes glowing slightly. They crinkled almost imperceptibly as he met Crane's gaze.

"Hello, Lord Crane. Thank you very much for coming. I wonder if you can give us a hand."

"By all means, Mr. Day." Crane wanted an apology for Stephen's latest disappearance, an explanation of how Rackham's greed really threatened him; he wanted to wind his fingers in the curly russet hair and pull the shorter man's head back for a kiss. He gave a small, polite smile instead. "In what way?"

"Well," Stephen said, "we need to speak to a practitioner urgently. Our usual interpreter is not available, and nobody appears to grasp what we're asking for, and these gentlemen don't want us to go any further, but I'm afraid that's not an option. I'd rather not force my way in, given a choice. The practitioners here are Mr. Bo and Mr. Tsang, and we need one of them as soon as possible."

"I'll see what I can do." Crane switched to Shanghainese, and spoke to the men carefully and reasonably for a few minutes, until it was clear that they had no intention of helping. At this point he raised his voice and lowered his tone.

"...and get him fucking *now*, you scrofulous, shit-stained syphilitic discards of a substandard brothel!" he bellowed after the three men who were fleeing out of the room, leaving one terrified guard flattening himself against the wall. He turned back to Stephen, whose expression was absolutely neutral. His colleagues looked somewhere between astonished and appalled, having understood his tone if not his words. The girl was grinning.

"They weren't very cooperative," Crane explained. "The shamans are unavailable, they said. They should be getting a headman, someone in authority, to tell me what the problem is."

"What are shamans?" asked the burly young man. He had a deep voice and an uncompromising look.

"A shaman is a Chinese practitioner," Stephen said. "Let me introduce you. Lord Crane, this is Peter Janossi, and Mrs. Esther Gold, and you've already met Jenny Saint."

Crane murmured courtesies and looked round at the urchin, realising that she must be the fourth of Stephen's team of justiciars. He had heard a certain amount about them all, and had pictured something rather more impressive than the reality. Janossi looked mildly hostile; Saint had what Crane suspected was a permanent smirk. Mrs. Gold was looking at him with interest, her head slightly cocked.

Crane knew from Stephen that Mrs. Gold was the senior member of the team, and that she resented the common assumption that she was subordinate to the men. He addressed his next words to her. "Please don't think this is vulgar curiosity, but if you want me to translate when someone arrives, it would help to know what I need to discuss. What's the problem?"

The practitioners glanced at each other, quick fleeting looks. Esther Gold said, "Rats."

"Rats?"

"Rats."

"We got a rat problem." Saint wore a malicious grin.

"I suppose you know you can hire a man and a dog in any pub in this city," Crane offered.

"It wouldn't help," Stephen said. "Joss, show him."

Janossi put a toe under a fold of the sackcloth bundle and flipped it over. Crane walked over and looked at what lay within.

It was undeniably a rat. Its long yellow teeth were bared in death. Its eyes were blood-filled and bulging, which Crane attributed to Stephen, since he had seen a man dead that way at his hands. Its matted, dirty brown pelt was stiff with filth and dust, its claws were grey and scaly, its naked tail pinkish. It was a rat like any other, except in one respect.

It was about four feet long, not counting the tail, and would have stood perhaps a foot high at the shoulder.

"I see," said Crane slowly. "No, I don't suppose a terrier would help, would it. Did you say *rat*, Mrs. Gold, or *rats*?"

"Rats."

"That's not good." Crane stared down at the monster. "How many?"

"Don't know," said Stephen. "At least twenty. And they appear to be normal rats apart from the size, so the answer to 'how many' is, for all we know, 'twice as many as yesterday'. It's been a busy morning," he concluded casually and met Crane's eyes for a second.

"You needn't let it concern you." Mrs. Gold sounded kind but firm. "We'll deal with this. Just help us speak to the practitioners here, and that will be all we ask of you."

Janossi nodded reassurance. Saint smirked. Stephen's gaze skittered up to the ceiling.

"Thank you," Crane said pleasantly. "Tell me, what makes you think this is a Chinese problem?"

"How do you mean?" asked Stephen.

"Why Limehouse, why shamans? Are you sure you're in the right place?"

"Why wouldn't we be?" demanded Janossi.

"Someone's coming," said Esther Gold, and they all looked round as a fat, elderly Chinese man bustled in.

"Ah!" he shouted. "Bamboo!"

CHAPTER SIX

Crane folded his arms and glared at Li Tang. He had known the man for many years in Shanghai, well enough for Li to use the old nickname that had once been so appropriate for an extraordinarily tall and thin youth. He had met him frequently in the last few months. They had ongoing business dealings. There was no reason at all for Li Tang to be utterly, uncompromisingly unhelpful.

"Why are you being such a complete bastard, my friend?" he enquired in a low voice.

Li Tang didn't respond to that. His face was stony.

"No shaman may be seen," he repeated for about the thirtieth time.

"By us or by anyone?"

"No shaman may be seen."

"Has Rackham been around?" Crane asked, drawing a bow at a venture.

Li Tang shrugged, apparently unmoved by the mention. "He wouldn't make a difference. No shaman may be seen."

"Since when are you a shaman's apprentice?" Crane enquired. "Don't you have other things to do than polish their rice bowls and make their appointments? Are you renouncing the world and your belly?"

"I speak with authority." Li Tang glowered at him.

"*You* speak with authority for shamans?" Crane raised his voice for the benefit of their audience, which currently numbered about eight Chinese as well as the British practitioners. "*You* decide who gets to see a shaman?"

Li Tang looked daggers at that. "I speak with authority."

"What are the names of your shamans?"

"That is not relevant."

"Mr. Bo and Mr. Tsang, is it? What are their full names?"

"You may not see them."

"I didn't ask that. I asked you to say their names." Crane dropped his voice low and saw the tiny twitch around Li's eyes. "Why won't you say their names?"

"My friend, this is not your business. So why don't you fuck off?"

"I'm just a translator for the British shamans," said Crane. "Why don't you tell them to fuck off? I'll watch. Even better, seeing as you and I are businessmen, why don't we both go do some business and leave the shamans to their own devices?"

"Today we are both mouthpieces," Li Tang countered. "And what my mouth is saying to you is that the shamans may not be seen. My advice, Bamboo, is that your ears should listen to what my mouth tells you."

"I hear what you're telling me, my fat friend," said Crane. "I hear it very clearly indeed."

He stalked back to the little group of justiciars.

"Well?" demanded Janossi.

"No play. Li Tang will be delighted to give you all possible assistance, short of a shaman, but I strongly suspect that assistance will be as much use as a glass hammer. They are not going to help."

"Yeah?" said Saint. "Well, that's their bloody problem, innit? Come on, we ain't having that, are we?"

"Surely not." Janossi looked to Esther and Stephen. "Let's just go in. Follow the rats, find where they're going and take it from there. Why the hell do we have to wait for permission in our own city?"

"We've spent years building a rapprochement with these people," Stephen said. "You know what happened with Arbuthnot last summer. If we go in mob-handed now—"

"They'll learn to cooperate next time!" Janossi interrupted, and wilted visibly under the look Stephen gave him.

Mrs. Gold was shaking her head. "I'm not seeing rapprochement here, Steph. And this problem is extending outside Limehouse, it's not just about them."

"Out of it, or into it?" asked Crane.

"What do you mean?"

"Are the rats coming from Limehouse, or emerging elsewhere and heading here?"

Esther Gold cocked her head to one side. "We don't know where they're coming from or going to. A number of them seemed to be coming here. We don't know any more, because we haven't managed to talk to any practitioners," she concluded pointedly. "And I think we should now go and look, Steph. I'm sorry if they don't like it, but this is British soil, not Chinese, people have died, and if they won't let us consult them, they don't get to be consulted."

Stephen gave a slight shrug of reluctant agreement and opened his mouth, and Crane said, "Just a moment."

"What?" Stephen asked. He frowned. "Is there a problem?"

"I'm not sure. Look, I wouldn't presume to tell you your business—"

"Bloody hope not!"

"That's enough, Saint," said Stephen. "But?"

Crane cast a glance over at Li Tang. "But China is my business, and—I really think it would be advisable to smile, and nod, and leave."

"*What?*" demanded Janossi.

Mrs. Gold looked as though she was running out of patience. "I don't know if you've forgotten, your lordship, but there is a giant rat on the floor in here, and a lot more out there, which somebody needs to do something about."

"I see the giant rat," Crane said. "And so did Li Tang, and he wasn't surprised to see it. I think you should leave now. I would."

"Why?"

"Can we talk about this later?"

"No, why don't you explain your reasoning now?" Esther's voice was hard.

Crane gave her a humourless smile. "Because I'd rather not share it with our friends over there."

"But nobody here speaks English—" Esther stopped abruptly. "Really. I *see*."

"Lord Crane," Stephen interjected. "Is that your professional opinion, that we would be well advised to leave? Because this is not a trivial matter. There are politics, and dead people."

"No, it isn't trivial. And yes, that's my professional opinion."

Stephen contemplated the taller man for a moment. Then he nodded and turned to the others. "All right. We're going. Lord Crane, tell the Chinese…I don't know, whatever you judge best. We will be back if need be."

"What?" said Janossi incredulously, as Esther said, "Excuse me?"

"I'm declaring this, Es," Stephen told her. "Follow my lead, please. We'll discuss it later."

Esther gave him a long, hard look and a reluctant nod. "Very well. Joss, get the rat."

Faced down and unsuccessful, the little group trooped out through the maze of corridors and alleys, back into the only relative airiness of the Limehouse streets.

Crane came out last and lengthened his stride to catch up with Esther and Stephen, who were engaged in a low-voiced, furious argument.

"Because he's not a fool, that's why!" Stephen was snapping.

"And he's not a practitioner either," Esther hissed back. "So what the devil does he have to say to it that makes his *opinion* worth more than mine?"

"Excuse me," Crane called, and both justiciars swung round. "Sorry to interrupt, but there's something that needs checking before we go further."

"There is no *we*." Esther spoke with barely restrained anger. "I appreciate your translation, but that is the limit of your involvement with this matter. This is not your business!"

"Let him speak, Es." Stephen sounded tired and irritated. "What is it, Lord Crane?"

"Does anyone know a good vantage point for rooftops around here? A tall tower or church spire?" Crane looked at the blank faces and added, "I don't know this part of Limehouse at all, and I want to see the roofs as soon as possible. There may not be much time."

"For what?" demanded Janossi.

"To test a theory."

"A *theory*?"

"Saint can get on the rooftops," Stephen said. "What should she look for?"

"Oh, for—" Esther span away, obviously fighting down a surge of temper.

"Look for flagpoles, Miss Saint," Crane told her. "Maybe one, possibly more. Standing proud of any nearby chimneys or walls, positioned to be visible. They may have several flags, they will definitely have long slender red pennants, and—can I borrow a pencil? Thanks. You may also see this symbol here on square red flags. When I say 'this symbol'," Crane added, with eight months' painful experience,

"I mean one exactly like that, rather than one which is also made up of some lines."

Saint gave him a malevolent look, but took the paper on which he'd sketched the character and slouched off down a nearby alley. The rest of them moved to the street corner, out of the path of walkers and shufflers. Janossi glared at a beggar till he went away.

Esther Gold looked after Saint, turned back to Crane with arms folded, and said, as one at the limits of her patience, "And may we know what flagpoles have to do with the serious problem that we're supposed to be dealing with at this moment?"

Crane glanced round. "I'd rather this wasn't overheard."

Stephen made a quick twitch of his fingers. The noise of the street was abruptly muted. "It won't be. Go on."

"The flagpoles she's looking for are ghost poles." Crane settled his shoulders back against a sun-warmed brick wall which was nevertheless still slightly clammy with long damp. "It's a very old shamanic practice. The idea is that when you die, while your body is prepared for burial, there is a chance that your soul will go wandering. If it can't find its way back to your body, it might become a hungry ghost or even take over someone else's body and become a *chiang-shih*, a vampire. So the ghost pole is put up where the body rests, to help your spirit find its way back."

"And whose perturbed spirit is in danger of getting lost?" asked Stephen.

Crane gave him a swift smile. "That's the thing. You see, ghost poles aren't usual these days, even in China. I doubt many people around here get the standard funerary rituals, let alone the ancient trappings. But there is one class of person for whom you would be insane not to erect a ghost pole. Even if you wanted their death an absolute secret, even if you were modern and enlightened, even if you barely believed in spirits at all, you would put up a ghost pole for them."

Esther was frowning slightly. "And they are?"

"Shamans," said Crane. "Practitioners. The lost souls of shamans make vampire ghosts of appalling evil and depravity. No offence."

There was a silence.

Janossi spoke first. "Are you pulling our legs?"

"No, he's not," Stephen said.

"You think the shamans are dead." Esther unfolded her arms. "That's why they wouldn't let us see them?"

"Li Tang wouldn't speak their names aloud, no matter how I pushed him, which is suggestive—it would attract the wandering soul's attention to name them while they're still unburied. And it is not Li Tang's, or anyone else's, place to control access to shamans. Shamans see whoever they want to. They don't hide away. Everything about the conversation I just had was wrong—unless he was trying to conceal that the men we were discussing were dead." Crane raised his hands. "I don't know. This is guesswork. I might be mistaken. But in my view, if that business had been intended simply as a snub, it would have been delivered in a way that left no room for other interpretation. My gut feeling is that you couldn't see the shamans because they aren't there to see."

"How recently would this have happened?" asked Esther.

Crane shrugged. "If the ghost poles are up, they'll have died within the last three days. That's all I can say. But, bear in mind, Li Tang wasn't just trying to bluff me, he was speaking to be heard by the people around him. I suspect he's under orders to keep it quiet. Are there other Chinese shamans here?"

"Not ones we've been permitted to meet. They don't deign to mix with us, apparently, but it's hard to say. Rackham was our only point of contact and he—" Stephen clearly changed what he was going to say. "He's not available for discussion."

"Here's Saint," said Esther.

The girl came sauntering round the corner a moment later, with a cocky little sneer, which evaporated as everyone turned to her and Esther demanded, "Well? Flagpoles?"

Saint nodded. "Two of 'em, looking like he said. What's this about?"

"Well, well, *well*." Stephen's eyes met Crane's for a second, glowing warm, and flicked away again. "Nicely done, my lord. And what do we suppose they died of?"

"Rats," said Janossi.

"Or a knife in the ribs," Crane suggested.

Esther's dark brows contracted. "Why?"

"It's why I wonder if you're looking in the right place. Look, will you all come back to my office? There's something else that you may need to know, and it might take a little while to explain. And I think we could use Merrick, my man, at this time."

"*My man?*" muttered Janossi.

"Be quiet, Joss," said Esther. "Lord Crane, if Saint identifies the addresses marked by the flagpoles, might we—you—be able to find out from the Chinese about the deaths, if they are practitioners, and what killed them?"

"I can try."

"Good. Saint, get back up there and find the flagpoles, and then meet us at Lord Crane's office. Do not even think about trying to act alone. Lead on, your lordship."

CHAPTER SEVEN

The building was empty except for Merrick when they arrived. Crane made brief introductions, and the two of them stood with the three justiciars in Crane's office, looking at the dead rat Janossi had dumped on the floor.

Merrick poked it thoughtfully with the toe of his boot. "Giant rats. Sumatra business, is this, my lord?"

"I don't know yet."

"What's Sumatra?" asked Janossi.

"A country, sir," Merrick said politely. "One of the Sunda islands. Go south from Kampuchea, you can't miss it. Is this to do with Mr. Willetts, my lord?"

"My question exactly."

"Feel free to explain." Stephen was sitting on the edge of the desk, legs dangling, and Crane was having a certain amount of trouble not thinking about his daydream of the other evening.

"It's a traveller's tale. Specifically, a tale told by David Willetts, a Java man. A trader, a wanderer and a chronic storyteller. By his account Sumatra is crawling with magic and evil priestly cults and enchantments and beautiful native sorceresses." Crane gave Esther a nod of acknowledgement. She gave him an incredulous glare. Stephen choked. "And it was from him that I, and Merrick, and pretty much everyone who ever had a drink with him, heard about the giant rats of Sumatra. Rats the size of dogs."

Stephen stopped swinging his legs. Esther steepled her fingers.

"I don't know many Java men," Crane went on. "So I don't know if this is a Willetts particular or a general legend—"

"I haven't heard it elsewhere," Merrick put in.

"No. As far as I know, the giant rats of Sumatra was Willetts' story. And the reason I bring it up is that Willetts is dead. He was murdered—knife in the ribs—in Poplar last week." Stephen whistled and exchanged a glance with Esther. "Now, it could be a coincidence that the one man in London who one would ask about giant rats has been murdered—"

"We don't like coincidences," Esther said. "Who killed him?"

"Unknown. He was stabbed and left by the river, as I heard."

"But lots of other people know the story, you said. So he wasn't killed to keep him quiet."

"Not to say *lots*, madam," Merrick offered. "Mr. Willetts didn't have a large acquaintance in England and his stories were, uh—"

"Not suitable for mixed audiences," Crane supplied. "Anyone at the Traders, the Far Eastern Mercantile club, would have heard it, anyone who drank with him, but it's not one he'd have rushed to tell in polite company."

Stephen frowned. "What is the story?"

"Don't mind me," Esther added. "I'm a married woman."

"It's fairly long. All right, let me try and remember the detail." Crane closed his eyes, calling back the memory of a hot night, warm sand underfoot, the sound of the sea. "Where were we, Merrick?"

"Hainan. Beach."

"That's right. We were drinking that stuff that smells of coconuts and tastes like hinge oil."

"Fermented whatnot. And he was trying to get rid of a load of copra on you, and you threw your shoe at a rat, and he said did we want to hear a story."

"That's it." Crane felt the memories open up. "It started with him in the jungle. He liked the jungle. He'd have hated to die by the Thames, poor swine."

"And he got lost," Merrick said. "Usual thing with Mr. Willetts. Canoe down a river and some rapids and two days' surviving alone in the heat, and all of that—"

"And he came across a village. The huts standing empty, cooking pots boiled dry over dead fires, no animals, no people. Strange marks on the trees and houses. Blood on the ground."

"So he sleeps there, like an idiot, and in the night there's men with spears and they blindfold him and take him to a cave."

"This is where it becomes very much a Willetts tale," Crane said. "In this cave, which is really an intricate system of caverns decorated with strange and ancient carvings, he meets a remarkably beautiful and barely dressed lady who is the high priestess of some deity. She falls in love with him more or less on sight, as so many beautiful native ladies did, according to him." He glanced at Esther. "We can probably miss out the next bit. The action picks up again as she explains that she is the…what was it…the vessel of the Red Tide, which serves to destroy anyone fool enough to defy her god. Now, there's also a priest, a huge native chap in a golden mask. He's jealous of Willetts' conquest, naturally."

"That's right," Merrick put in. "And the gold-mask bloke makes a fuss, and there is some stuff about her duty to the god, and then some shenanigans about a serving maid what *also* falls in love with Mr. Willetts, only this is actually a setup by the gold-mask bloke to annoy the priestess lady, right?"

"Dear God," Stephen said. "How much of this is there?"

"You're getting the abridged version," Crane told him. "Willetts could keep this one going all night, including the interludes with the priestess, and the serving maid, and the priestess *and* the serving maid."

Esther's eyebrows shot up. "Feel free to miss out that part too."

"So, anyway, what it boils down to is, the priestess calls the Red Tide on Mr. Willetts and the maid, right?" Merrick went on. "Only the maid's seen this coming, cos she's fallen in love with Mr. Willetts for real by now"—Esther sighed heavily—"and she's given him a thingy what will save him from it."

"An amulet belonging to the gold-mask priest chap," Crane amplified.

"And the Red Tide comes, and what it is is this whole load of giant rats."

"Dozens and hundreds of rats, in a furry, flowing, stinking, snarling tide." Crane remembered this part vividly. "They flow over the maid and the golden-mask chap and strip them to the bone with tooth and claw. They knock Willetts down too, but he's unharmed because of the amulet. He really went to town on what it felt like, having these great heavy animals all over him, bare tails lashing him, the smell and the coarse wet belly hair rubbing over his face, and the claws treading and flattening over him. It was very convincing."

"It was good, yeah," Merrick agreed. "So eventually the lady finishes up, and the rats move off, and Mr. Willetts ain't dead but the golden chappy is. And…what happens then?"

"She declares undying love, which he returns, and then he wakes up next to her cold corpse because some other priest has strangled her in her sleep."

Merrick was shaking his head. "No, that's not it. What it was, she wanted Mr. Willetts to take the mask and be the new god bloke. And when he says no, she summons the guards, and Mr. Willetts accuses her of blasphemy, and he has it away on his toes while the guards strangle her."

"How on earth do you get those mixed up?" asked Stephen.

"Oh, the ending changed a few times," Crane said. "When a chap was telling it in the Traders the other night, she renounced her duties to run away with Willetts, and before she could get on a ship with him a killer came for her, sent by the betrayed god. She always died, though."

"Funny, now you say that," said Merrick. "His ladies usually just pined after him, in the stories. They didn't usually die."

"Anyway. That's it, in a very large nutshell."

"It's not, perhaps, the most plausible story I've ever heard," said Stephen. "Points of interest, though."

"By God there are," said Janossi.

Esther nodded slowly. "How much truth would you say was in this?"

Crane shrugged. "Willetts travelled a lot, and strange things happen more openly in that part of the world. That said, he was an awful liar about women. But in general, I'd say he embroidered stories, rather than making things up of whole cloth."

"He told the one about the crabman pretty much as it happened," Merrick offered.

"He *what*?"

Merrick grinned unsympathetically. "What, you thought he'd keep a story like that quiet? But he was spot on with it, as I recall."

"That…individual can count himself lucky he's dead," said Crane. "And I'll speak to you later, you turncoat. Anyway. It's possible that some of the story was accurate, but what and how much is anyone's guess."

Esther frowned. "How did the priestess call the Red Tide? How much detail did he go into?"

"That I don't remember. It would doubtless have been a fair bit, he had an astonishing memory, but I don't. Merrick?"

Merrick shook his head. "Chanting, was it? Singing?"

"When you say an astonishing memory…" Stephen began.

"Very good indeed. He picked up languages like nobody's business. Terrific ear."

"Good enough to remember and repeat, say, a chant, if he had heard one?"

"Perhaps."

Esther nodded. "And what happened to the amulet?"

"No idea."

"How did the rats leave? Where did they go?"

"I don't recall anything about that."

"Or where they came from?"

"Sorry. If Willetts put it in the story, I've forgotten."

Janossi made a disgusted noise. "The one man we need to speak to, and he's dead. And that's why he's dead, of course."

"Likely, certainly," said Stephen. "Well, now. Giant rats used as a weapon. A method of calling them. A protective amulet. The man who might know the call or own the amulet stabbed to death down in Poplar last week."

"Rats springing up through the East End and heading into Limehouse," Esther continued. "Two dead Chinese practitioners."

"And a houseful of corpses on Ratcliffe Highway," Janossi finished grimly. "Chance, or someone trying out a new toy?"

"There's a thought," said Esther. "Here's Saint coming."

There was a banging at the front door a few seconds later. Merrick let the girl in, and Esther gave her a rapid summary of events. As they spoke, Crane edged over to Stephen and propped himself on the desk.

"Interesting day?"

"As you see. Thank you for this. I thought you'd help but I didn't expect quite such a contribution."

"I am forever at your service," said Crane lightly, and felt Stephen's eyes flick to him.

"Well, I'm in your debt," he returned equally lightly. "Please do collect."

"I shall." Crane allowed just a hint of promise into his voice. "So you think Willetts' tale was more than a lot of tommyrot?"

"His murder lends it credibility. Of course it might just be coincidence, but you know how I feel about that."

"You spurn it as you would a rabid dog."

Stephen grinned up at him, then looked over at the others. "All right, everyone, plan of action. We need to find out how the shamans died and if it's linked to the rats; we need to find out more about Willetts' death; most crucially, we need to look for evidence of whether the rats are appearing at random or being called. Are there many Sumatrans in London, Lord Crane?"

"Not that I know of. The odd sailor, perhaps, not a big migrant settlement."

"Is Sumatra the same as China?" asked Saint.

"No," said Merrick and Crane, simultaneously and emphatically. Merrick added, "Couple thousand miles off. Different people. Different language."

"Does either of you speak Sumatran?" Esther put in.

"Malay. No, but Merrick's not bad with pidgin. Then again, anyone surviving over here will speak English, there's not a lot of Malay spoken this side of the globe."

Stephen nodded. "Saint, did you find the addresses? Good. Mr. Merrick, can I borrow you to look into what happened to the shamans?"

"Be a pleasure, sir."

"Thank you. Saint, take Mr. Merrick to the flagpole houses and back him up. Subtly, please. Do not get into trouble."

"That goes for you too," Crane told Merrick.

"Esther?"

"I'm going to Ratcliffe Highway for a sniff around. If this is a deliberate summoning, that might have been a practice run, in which case I'll bet the summoner was near. Joss, with me, unless you need him, Steph?"

"No, I think I'll look into Mr. Willetts' death," Stephen said. "The sooner we find out if this was a deliberate summoning, the better. Lord Crane, if you're not busy—"

"I can take you to the Traders," Crane offered. "There are a few Java men there, they'll know as much as anyone in England about Willetts. And a few scholarly types who might know something about Sumatran legends and so on."

"Perfect." Esther clapped her hands. "Lord Crane, thank you very much. I needn't tell you to keep this quiet, need I? All right, Saint, gentlemen, meet tomorrow, surgery, ten, unless anything goes catastrophically wrong before then. Everyone moving please."

"Let me lock up here, Mr. Day, and I'll take you to the Traders." Crane moved to close the shutters as the others left.

When the outside door shut behind the last of them, he slid the bolt through and felt Stephen's arms go round his waist.

"Hello." He twisted round and slipped his hands under Stephen's shabby jacket.

"Hello to you." Stephen leaned forward, resting his head against Crane's chest. "And thank you. You're rather marvellous."

"Says the man with magic hands." Crane brushed his own slender, ordinary fingers through Stephen's curls. "When did you leave this morning?"

"About four. I'd have stayed if I could, but these blasted rats."

"What happened on Ratcliffe Highway?"

Stephen's arms tightened slightly. "They attacked a boarding house three days ago. A lot of rats. Twenty or more, according to the survivors."

"Survivors. Who died?"

"Anyone who couldn't get out. A lace-maker, her infant, her two-year-old, a sailor with a wooden leg, a consumptive. The rats somehow got through the cellar door and went up through the house like a, well, a tide. Everyone who could run did so. By the time they went back in, the rats had gone, and there were five chewed bodies."

"Jesus. Why wasn't that in the broadsheets?"

Stephen shrugged one shoulder. "There's, shall we say, a policy against causing alarm with stories of this sort. People would rather not hear it. The survivors are being treated for fever, or a bad batch of gin, or something like that, and the deaths ascribed to a mad dog, I think."

"The witnesses are being told they didn't see it?" said Crane, incredulously.

"Told it didn't happen as they thought. It might be a relief for some of them to believe that. I don't know. I don't know if the poor swine who came back home to find his wife and children dead might take some comfort from the idea they weren't ripped to shreds by giant rats." Stephen swallowed. "I saw his face, Lucien. The policeman telling him his family was dead, and that he couldn't see the bodies. He'd got a new job just that day. He was coming home to tell his wife. He had some sweetmeats in a basket, for the children."

"God."

"We thought it was an accident. Some freak occurrence. Escaped pets or experiments or what have you. That was bad enough. If they were summoned, if this was deliberate rather than chance…"

"Mrs. Gold said a practice run," Crane said. "Practice at what?"

"Trying out the control over the rats, I imagine. Bring them out, call them back. Watch them kill."

"Ratcliffe Highway is a fairly busy place for magical experiments."

"Mmm," said Stephen. "I was wondering if that was a joke. Ratcliffe."

"If it was, I trust you'll be making the joker laugh on the other side of his face."

"Only if Esther doesn't get to him first. She has no sense of humour." Stephen held on to Crane for a moment longer, then let out a long breath. "Before we go to this club of yours, do we need to discuss Rackham?"

"Let me handle that."

Stephen stilled. He moved back a couple of steps so he could look up at Crane. "I'm not a child, Lucien. Rackham is as much my problem as yours. And I don't need your protection."

"No, you need to eliminate a plague of giant killer rats, and find out if some murderous bastard called it up. So you concentrate on that, and I'll take Rackham off your plate while you do it."

Stephen stared up a minute longer, then his shoulders dropped slightly. "I see what you're saying, but—"

Crane sighed. "It is actually possible to accept help without marking yourself as a weakling, you know."

Stephen flushed. "I'm perfectly capable of accepting help. I asked you to come today, didn't I? And look what happened."

"What?" said Crane, injured.

"We discovered we may have two dead shamans and a rat-controlling maniac at large. Whereas if you hadn't been there, I might have given up and gone home early." Stephen moved into Crane's arms again. "I'm sorry, Lucien. And I'm sorry about last night, too, I wasn't very fair to you. I'm a bag of nerves at the moment. Do I need to dress up like a shop dummy for this club?"

"Not by normal human standards. Which is to say, yes, my sweet, you do. Why don't you come back to the flat to get some decent clothes, and I'll see if I can do something for your nerves while I'm at it?"

"Mmm. Tempting. Though…"

Stephen hopped backwards to sit on the desk and Crane moved between his legs to kiss him, felt him lean back invitingly, and grinned against his mouth. "Dear me, Mr. Day. You really do love to get fucked on desks, don't you? Put you on a desk, and you're begging for it. What is so particularly exciting about desks?"

"They're not exciting, they're boring." Stephen quivered as Crane's mouth moved to his sensitive earlobes. "You write on them and then you go home, and nothing horrible happens, nobody dies. Lovely dull surfaces. All the better to do interesting things on." He slid his electric hands down Crane's back, over his hips.

"There's a perfectly good desk in the flat," Crane said. "A lot stronger than this, and decidedly safer."

"*But*, in the Strand," Stephen argued, "whereas this desk is right here, and you could have me on it right now."

"You're feeling more yourself, I see."

Stephen locked his arms round Crane's neck, wrapped his legs round the other's hips, and lifted himself clear off the desk to press their bodies together. Crane staggered at his weight and braced himself with his hands, laughing.

"I have wanted this since you called Esther a beautiful native sorceress." Stephen started laughing too. "Her face, my God. You're such a swine."

"And you love it."

Stephen grinned, then moved to meet Crane's lips in a long, deep kiss that ended with him on his back on the desk and Crane half on top of him, painfully erect. "I need to lock the door," Crane said throatily. "Unless you can do it from here."

"Iron," Stephen said with concision; Crane was well aware iron was unresponsive to his powers. "But I bet I can get naked before you can lock the door and get back."

"Stakes?"

"Ooh. If I win we do it on the desk. If you win, you can have me against the wall."

That was a worthwhile wager. Crane loved to screw against walls but the height difference made it necessary for Stephen to stand on something, and while he was normally unconcerned by his stature, that did annoy him. "You're on."

He lost, of course, since Stephen cheated ruthlessly by sending the keys flying from his hand and skidding across the floor, but as he buried himself in Stephen's body and felt those magic hands flare joyously against his back while Stephen's teeth dug into his shoulder, he felt as if he had won a victory of another and much more important kind, though he would have been hard-pressed to say what it was.

CHAPTER EIGHT

A couple of hours later, Crane sat at ease in the Traders. Stephen was next to him, wearing the suit Crane had bought him. Stephen's obvious poverty, added to the height difference, made a mismatch in their appearances that drew far more attention than was prudent, and since Crane was an extraordinarily rich man where Stephen struggled to pay the rent, it had seemed only sensible to him that he should fund a decent set of clothes. Stephen had reluctantly accepted that, but had reacted with fury when he learned that Crane had had several other suits made up for him at the same time. He would have been livid had he known quite how obscenely expensive the discreet tailoring establishment was.

Anyone who cared about clothes would have known, Crane reflected. The material he'd selected, with no help from his sartorially inexperienced lover, was a subtle heather mix with tiny flecks of red and yellow, a quiet, autumnal effect that set off Stephen's hair and eyes perfectly, and it was flatteringly cut, without any ostentatious attempt to make up for his lack of height or breadth. He looked, Crane thought, delightful: well dressed, bright-eyed and freshly fucked, the latter point hopefully lost on the men gathered around the table with them.

They were in the Traders' conversation room for postprandial drinks. Cryer was there, with one speculative eye on the attractive young man who had arrived with Crane; Humphris, abstracted and frowning; and Peyton, interjecting obvious sarcasm whenever he could. Shaycott was enthusiastically retelling Willetts' Red Tide tale yet again, but had earned his keep by introducing a Java man named Oldbury who Crane hadn't met before, and a scholarly type called Dr. Almont, who he had seen haunting the library on several occasions, and who was apparently an expert on Polynesian tradition insofar as that was possible without ever having left England.

Shaycott came to the much-anticipated end of his tale and got a minimal grunt of appreciation from most of those present and an enthusiastic response from Stephen.

"What a marvellous yarn, thank you, sir. Is that a common legend in those parts, I wonder, the rat cult?"

"Not that I heard," Oldbury said. "Only ever had it from Willetts."

"It has some similarities to other tales in the tropes of the priestess and the summoning." Dr. Almont settled down to lecture. "Interestingly, it lacks an element one would have expected, which may be found in many superficially similar tales, the device or motif of the *anitu*."

"Ghost," said Oldbury.

"More than merely a ghost, if I may say so. The *anitu*, or spirit of the dead that has the capacity to animate another body—"

"Not in this one," Oldbury said firmly. "No ghosts, just rats."

"How much truth would you say there was in this?" Crane asked.

"Truth!" Peyton snorted. "Giant rats and lovely darkies! Honestly, Vaudrey—"

"Crane. *Lord* Crane."

Peyton flushed. "Willetts was a shocking liar. His stories were all absolute rubbish. You should know. He had the most marvellous tale about you."

"If you mean the one about the crabman, it is, unfortunately, quite accurate." The chorus of incredulous mockery that erupted suggested

Willetts had shared the story widely. Crane spared an unkind thought for the deceased trader and waited for the catcalls to die down. "Yes, well, I was horribly drunk. These things happen."

"They don't happen to anyone else." Monk looked amused for the first time that evening.

"Oh, I don't know. I always thought things happened to Willetts."

Oldbury gave a grunt of agreement. "Ready for any spree. Looked for adventure."

"And when one looks for adventure, one often finds it. *I've* seen some strange sights—" Shaycott began.

Crane came in over him ruthlessly. "We all have. Did you ever see this rat amulet of his, Oldbury?"

The Java man shrugged. "Any amount of stuff. Rooms packed with it."

"What's happening to his things?" Crane asked. "Who's his next of kin? Did he even have family over here?"

"Sister. Why he came back. Sick, you know. Lungs."

"Poor chap," Crane said, frowning. "Do you have her direction, at all? I'd like to send my condolences."

The conversation splintered up into groups. Crane ensured he was with Oldbury and Humphris, finding out what he could about Willetts' murder without seeming too obvious. He didn't get much. After half an hour or so he looked around for Stephen, who had taken the unenviable task of talking to Dr. Almont. The scholar was still there, now latched on to Shaycott, but Stephen was gone.

"Looking for your pal?" asked Town, at his elbow.

"He probably jumped from the window," said Crane. "Almont is a shocking dullard, isn't he?"

Town rolled his eyes. "He and Shaycott won't shut up, and Oldbury talks as though he was charged by the word. I don't know what it is about Java men. Bores, every last one. Except Willetts. You have an interest there?"

"Not particularly. Just rather sorry for the poor fellow, wondered if I might help his sister. Day's the one interested in Java."

"Your little, ah, friend?" Town waggled his eyebrows.

"You have the wrong end of the stick, I'm afraid," said Crane. "Since I'm not getting any of the stick at all, if you follow me." Town, who loved a filthy joke, spluttered into his whisky. "He's a friend of one of my cousins, got some kind of interest in the place. Not my bag, but I can play the head of the family by palming him off on Shaycott and Almont, and if he's grateful enough, who knows, the palming off may not stop there."

"Hah! Well, good hunting, my dear fellow," said Town, with comfortable callousness. "Though I don't rate your chances if Peyton's buttonholing him with stories of your disgraceful doings. He followed him out a few minutes back."

"Blast. Oh well, it was a long shot. Have you seen Rackham recently?"

Apparently Town hadn't, nor did he have any new gossip to offer. They chatted a little longer. Stephen didn't reappear when Peyton did, but some time later a waiter brought a note which Crane read, then stuffed into his pocket.

Peyton was watching. "Bad news, *Lord* Crane? I do hope your plans for the evening haven't been spoiled for any reason."

"Trivial," said Crane.

Merrick got back to the flat some half an hour after Crane, looking decidedly the worse for wear.

"Fun evening?"

"You might say." Merrick tried to hang up his hat, and missed. "You got any idea what that Miss Saint can do?"

"Drink a grown man under the table, apparently. Did you find out about the shamans?"

"Yeah. It was rats."

"No trouble?"

"Not to speak of," Merrick said. "You?"

"Not much success. And the Amazing Vanishing Shaman has buggered off again, without a word, as usual." Crane's tone wasn't quite as light as he'd intended.

"Cor, dear." Merrick shook his head. "You have got it bad, ain't you?"

"Shut up."

"I'm just saying. Round his little finger."

"Shut up."

"Pining, that's what you are. I didn't recognise it at first, but—"

"Shut *up*, you repulsive inebriate, or I will dismiss you without a character. And go to bed. We're up early tomorrow."

"Gawd, are we? Why?"

"Rackham," said Crane. "He gave me till Friday and that's tomorrow. So we're going to see him first thing."

"He won't be up first thing."

"He will once I've dragged him out of bed. Leo Hart sent me a note, he's asked her for five hundred pounds. She's fairly upset. And since we've got nowhere finding anything good on him, we're going to have to act a bit more directly."

"Good-oh. What we going to do?"

"Break his legs, I suppose," Crane said. "Or offer him five hundred quid to fuck off. Or both."

"Better not break his legs if you want him to fuck off on 'em. What's Mr. Day say?"

"He's got troubles of his own. I want Rackham to stop being one of them."

"Yeah, you take charge of that." Merrick yawned widely. "Gawd knows he can't handle himself. And you never know, do enough stuff for him, he might stick around a bit longer."

"What the hell does that mean?"

Merrick gave him a look. "Means you need to do a bit more thinking, that's what. You reckon if I was a Long Meg like you, I'd act like I ruled the world too?"

"I do not act like I rule the world, and what's my height got to do with anything?" Crane snapped. "What brought this on?"

"You work it out. I'm going to bed."

"Fuck you too," said Crane, and stalked off in a thoroughly bad mood.

He was still in a foul temper the next morning as they knocked at the door of Rackham's lodging house. It was off Cable Street in a rather miserable area of town east of the Tower. The house was damp, the landlady not overwhelmingly respectable or polite. She was torn between contempt for anyone who wanted to see her unloved lodger and awe at Crane's obvious wealth.

"Well, I dare say you can go straight in then, sir," she muttered, pocketing the generous tip Crane offered for her trouble. "You'll be lucky to find him up. Lazy worthless piece of trouble, that man is, with his dirty friends."

Crane and Merrick followed her through the low door, through a dank and cabbage-redolent corridor, and up an ill-swept landing, where she left them with something close to a flounce, and a suggestion that Crane could mention the matter of this month's rent to Rackham while he was there.

"Well, he's not spending his ill-gotten gains on luxurious living." Crane banged on the door.

Merrick hunched his shoulders. "He deaf or what? That racket's giving me a headache."

"No, that was you getting sloshed with a small child."

"Barely had a drop. God, she can drink, that one."

"Stephen too," Crane said. "It doesn't seem to touch the sides. Must be a practitioner thing. What did you mean, last night, about me thinking I rule the world?"

"Did I say that? Must have been trollied."

"You were. What did you mean?"

Merrick looked at him out of one eye, assessing. "Yeah, well, maybe not rule the world, as such…"

"What, then? Come on, spit it out. I want to know."

"If you say so, my lord. You're bloody tall. And you're rich, and you ain't stupid, mostly, and there's people reckon you're not bad looking, which *I* got no opinion on, and your old man was an earl and that shows. It always did."

"Right, you've met me," Crane said. "So?"

Merrick rolled his eyes. "So, what I'm saying is, you might think you're treating someone as an equal, but you ain't. Because, my lord earl, when you're bigger and older and richer and all that *and* you're naturally a domineering sod, maybe that person don't feel equal, no matter what you might reckon. I don't mean me," he added, in case Crane should get the wrong idea.

Crane moved closer and lowered his voice. "I may be all those things but I'm not a magician. Christ, you've seen what he can do, and you're telling me *he* feels intimidated by *me*? He scares the hell out of me!"

"Does he know that?" said Merrick. "I mean, he's a shaman, but he's only human. No family. On his own. Always has to watch his back. And then along you come, with all that stuff I said, plus you don't give a shit about anyone knowing you like blokes. The biggest problem he's got and for you it's *nothing*. He's terrified, you couldn't give a monkey's. And you're all, like, 'I'll buy this, I'll dress you, I'll fix it, I'm in charge—'"

"Shut up," said Crane. "Enough."

"I ain't saying you do it on purpose. But that bloke's held together by spit and pride, and if you take away his pride—"

"I heard you, damn it. Stop."

Merrick shrugged and leaned back against the wall. Crane stared at nothing for a few minutes, then banged savagely on the door again. "Is this bastard ever going to open up?"

"Look, sod this," said Merrick. "Shall I open it for him?"

"Oh, why not. If he's not in, we'll leave a message. If he is in, it's my turn first."

Crane positioned himself to obscure Merrick from the view of anyone who might come up the stairs while his henchman got to work on the lock with a piece of bent metal he produced from his pocket. It took him no more than five or six seconds, then he stepped back with an "after you" gesture, and Crane turned the handle and opened the door.

The smell hit first. It was threefold: something musty and animal; the familiar stench of shit and piss; and the sharp iron tang of blood. A lot of blood.

"Fuck," said Merrick, as they stood in the doorway and stared into the slaughterhouse of Rackham's room. "*Fuck.*"

There was blood on the walls. It was smeared to about a foot off the ground, spattered higher up. It was smeared on the floor too, as if low furry bellies had dragged through the pools, with sharp snakelike curves where tails had flicked, and unmistakable long-toed footprints.

Rackham's sandy hair was still visible on top of his scalp, but there wasn't much else left that was recognisable.

"Jesus Christ." Crane shut the door again.

"I don't reckon we can slip off," Merrick said quietly, in Shanghainese. "The landlady will give a description."

"Of course she will. Shut up a moment." Crane bit his lip. "Right. I'll stay. You go find a policeman. And then—do you remember that address Stephen gave you, back at Piper, for Mrs. Gold? Her husband's surgery?"

"Devonshire Street." It had been four months ago, but Merrick had the retentive memory of the barely literate.

"Good man. Go there. They said they were meeting there at ten. If you happen to find Stephen alone, talk to him and follow his lead, but if not, this is important, *tell them anyway.* Don't wait to talk to him.

And listen: *I'm* being blackmailed by Rackham. Not Stephen, nothing to do with Stephen. You aren't going to tell Mrs. Gold that because it's none of her business, but that's your story to keep in mind, got it? So everything you do has to flow from that. We've found Rackham dead, so you've got the police and gone straight off to tell the shamans about rats, and you don't care which of them you talk to on that, because Stephen is nothing to do with this or me or anything. Understand?"

"Got you. There something I should know?"

"He's in trouble with his colleagues," Crane said shortly. "I'll tell you later. Go, and don't talk to the landlady, send her up."

CHAPTER NINE

The landlady did not take the news well. She was still having hysterics when a policeman came in. He took one look at the charnel scene in Rackham's room and vomited on the landing, which scarcely improved the choking atmosphere. By the time an inspector arrived, Crane was ready to damn Rackham's soul to hell for dying in such an aggressively unpleasant manner.

Inspector Rickaby was at least competent. A weary-looking man with a neat moustache, he contemplated the slaughter with a look of mild disgust, and poked around the gobbets of flesh and splintered bone as though he saw shredded people on a daily basis.

They sat in the small shabby parlour, and he listened to Crane's account with an expression of patient interest.

"So, my lord, you were merely here to visit a friend?"

"That's right."

Inspector Rickaby turned Crane's card over and back as though he expected to find a clue on it. "Earl Crane. Shouldn't there be an 'of' in that?"

"No. It's like Earl Grey."

"The tea?"

"The lord."

"Ah. Do you suppose Earl Grey has many friends in Wapping?"

"I've no idea. I've never met the man."

"I just wondered. If earls usually have friends in these parts of London."

"I couldn't speak for other earls," said Crane. "I have several friends in this part of London. I lived in China between the ages of seventeen and thirty-seven, Inspector, and I only came back to England eight months ago. Most of my acquaintances in this country are either Chinese or old China hands. People very like Rackham."

"But not dead, I hope."

"No, most of them aren't dead at all."

The inspector tilted his head. "Good friend, was he?"

"I knew him for a long time."

"You don't seem upset."

"I'm reasonably upset. I just found him in small pieces."

"Most distressing, my lord. Was the deceased expecting you?"

"He was, but not at a specific time," Crane said. "I'd promised him a loan. I came here on my way to my office to drop off the money."

"But he didn't answer the door when you knocked."

"For obvious reasons."

"So how did you get in?"

"I opened it. It was unlocked."

Rickaby nodded. "Again, my lord, forgive my ignorance, but as an earl, would you normally go round trying people's doors on the off chance? Because most of us, if our friends don't answer the door, we walk away, we don't see if we can let ourselves in."

Crane paused, attempting to give the air of a man with a moral dilemma, then spoke frankly. "Inspector, you'll understand that I'd rather this didn't get about more than it has to, but Mr. Rackham was an opium addict. It was entirely usual for him not to lock his door. I expected to find him asleep in bed, I wanted to drop off the money and get to work, so I tried the door, and found—as you saw."

"Do you have many friends who are opium addicts, my lord? As an earl?"

"As a China man, yes, I do."

"Who do you think killed him?"

"An animal. Or a lunatic."

"An opium addict?"

Crane pretended to think about that. "Possible, I suppose."

"Do you take opium, my lord?"

"No, Inspector, I don't. Nor do I butcher people."

"No need to be defensive, my lord, I'm just asking the questions. Now—what is it, Gerrard? Can't you see I'm busy?" Rickaby glared at the young constable standing just inside the door.

"Yes, sir. I'm sorry, sir. It's them, sir."

"Them? Which *them* is that, lad?"

"The funny ones, sir."

The inspector's face stilled. Then he said, "Where are they?"

"Up there, sir, in the room. Sorry, sir. Not sure how they got past Motley, sir."

Rickaby took a deep breath. "Well, why don't you ask them to come down here, then."

"No need." Esther Gold strode into the parlour. There was blood on the hem of her long skirt. Stephen followed. He had dark patches on his knees and was wiping his hands on an unpleasantly stained handkerchief. His glance flicked over Crane, showing no recognition. "A word, please, Inspector."

The word took several minutes. Crane waited in the hallway, as requested, taking the opportunity to marshal his thoughts and prepare his story. The inspector had been uncomfortably perspicacious, evidently sensing something off about Crane's account of events, and although his spotless clothing surely absolved him from serious accusation, his relations with Rackham would not bear close investigation.

Finally the door opened. "Up to you, Mrs. Gold," said Rickaby, as he prepared to walk out. "But you know my mind."

"Thank you," came Esther's voice as the inspector passed Crane without a word. "Lord Crane, could you come in?"

Crane shut the door behind him, facing Esther and Stephen. "I feel like a schoolboy coming in to see the Head. What's happening?"

"We've asked the police to leave the investigation to us," Stephen said. "Rickaby's not very happy."

"Can you do that?"

"Yes," said Esther. "Tell me what happened."

"I came to see Rackham. He was dead. That's it. I saw nothing that isn't still there. I sent Merrick for the police and for you."

"The inspector told us his door was unlocked," Esther commented. Stephen said nothing, didn't look at Crane. He was paler than usual.

Crane made sure he addressed Esther. "No, it was locked. Merrick picked it for me. I didn't share that with Rickaby. I felt a locked-door mystery was more than he needed."

"I dare say. Why did you break into his room?"

"Because I wanted to talk to him. I thought he was either doped or ignoring me on purpose."

"Why did you want to talk to him?"

"This is sounding not unlike an interrogation," Crane observed. "And I'm reasonably sure I don't come under your jurisdiction."

"Here's my problem," Esther said. "How many of you old China hands and Java men are there in London? All these people who lived on the other side of the world and know each other?"

"I don't know. A couple of hundred, all told?"

"Mmm. And a week ago one of you is stabbed, and another kills himself, and now a third is ripped to shreds by rats, just like two more Chinese down in Limehouse. Would you normally expect to lose three members of your club by violence in less than a fortnight?"

"Not usually, no."

"So, three dead men. And a fourth man who belongs to the same club, who is there when we're finding out about more men killed by rats, who picks a lock to find a body—"

"Ah, no, wait a moment," said Crane. "I see your thinking, but you're making a logical error."

"Am I?"

"Yes. You're looking at my involvement with Rackham as a factor, whereas it's more like a condition. I met Mr. Day because I knew Rackham. Mr. Day asked me to help yesterday because he knew me through Rackham. I came here this morning on an unrelated matter, because I knew Rackham. The coincidence—I know that's not a popular word—lies with Rackham's involvement with rats, not mine with Rackham."

Esther didn't look convinced. "You came to see him by pure chance, picking a lock to do it."

Crane ignored that. He was trying not to look at Stephen, but peripheral vision was showing him a very white face, and he could almost feel the younger man's sickening tension. If Stephen felt this was necessary for the investigation, he would speak, Crane knew it, and he willed him to be silent a little longer. Merrick's words were buzzing in his brain, but this was something he could shape and Stephen couldn't, and surely that was only sensible. "Look, Mrs. Gold, I'll grant you the rats tie Rackham and Willetts together, but as to Merton's suicide and my involvement... Assuming the other death you mean is Merton?"

"Yes," said Stephen colourlessly.

"You think it's coincidence that another of your friends killed himself a week ago, just before all this?" Esther interjected.

"Merton was no friend of mine." Crane paused deliberately. "I don't have any idea of what's going on here. But, in case it's relevant, I will tell you this. Rackham was a blackmailer."

Stephen gave a tiny gasp. Esther said, "Rackham?"

"Yes. I don't know if he was blackmailing Merton, but I assume so. I know that he was attempting to blackmail at least two other people. Both China hands, like Merton, like Rackham."

"Like you?"

"Exactly like me," said Crane calmly. "I came here with the intention of beating him to a pulp, only to find him very obviously dead by rat. I can't say I mourn his passing."

"Did you tell Rickaby this?"

"Good God, no."

"What hold did Rackham have over you?"

"Esther!" yelped Stephen.

"Nothing that worried me. I'm afraid my profound lack of interest in my family name makes me a terrible subject for extortion."

"Is that so. But presumably Rackham knew that," said Esther. "So why did he try?"

Crane shrugged as casually as he could. "He probably hoped I'd throw him a few quid to go away. I might even have done." Esther kept looking at him, dark eyes intent, nostrils slightly flaring. Crane concentrated on keeping his body relaxed, not filling the silence.

Esther spoke first. "Who else was he blackmailing?"

"I'm not telling you that. I only know of one other person, and that individual is not a practitioner, has nothing to do with any of this, and has suffered quite enough insult at Rackham's hands already."

"What makes you think the Pied Piper is a practitioner?" asked Esther.

"What?"

"It's what we're calling the summoner." Stephen's voice sounded slightly thin to Crane's ears. "Pied Piper. Rats."

"Yes, I grasp that. How could it not be a practitioner?"

"It depends on the method used," Stephen said. "But it could quite possibly be someone with latent talent or very limited powers. Someone we don't know about."

Crane digested that. "So it could be anyone who knew Willetts' story, who'd learned the incantation or had hold of this amulet?"

"Anyone who knew Willetts well, and who wanted Rackham and two Chinese practitioners dead." Esther raised a brow. "Can you think of anyone like that?"

"According to Rackham, neither of those shamans spoke English," Stephen added. "So whoever wanted them dead must have been involved with China, to have any connection with them."

"I see," said Crane slowly, mind racing. "I see."

"I don't suppose it was you." Esther spoke reasonably. "You brought Willetts and the dead practitioners to our attention, after all. But I think you will have to tell us everything you know about who Rackham was blackmailing."

"No."

Esther took a step forward. Crane took two rapid steps back. "If you're thinking about putting fluence on me, *don't*." He heard the note of something like panic in his voice. He loathed the very idea of fluence, hated the idea of having someone magically tamper with his mind ever again, but even more, he knew he couldn't risk the loss of control, for Stephen's sake or his own.

Esther's brows were raised. "How do you know about fluence?"

"I fluenced him." Stephen stood behind her, voice unhappy. "And I shouldn't have, and I swore I wouldn't do it again. Or let anyone else do it."

"Well, that was silly of you," she observed.

"Possibly. Don't, Es. I can't let you. I made a promise."

Esther looked round at him. Stephen shrugged. "Sorry. It wouldn't help anyway—" He stumbled over the words, stopping himself abruptly.

"Why not?" asked Esther.

"Because… Rackham had his fingers in too many pies. Well, you know, we had to stop using him to translate, he was getting more and more unreliable. I'm not saying the blackmail isn't what got him killed but for someone making a mess of things on the scale he was, I am actually prepared to look at coincidence for once. Anyway, look, Es, we're wasting time, and there's at least two more pressing issues, one of which is to do with some of the people I met at the Traders last night, and the other is how the rats got in."

He had said most of that too fast, to Crane's ear, and had signally failed to answer the original question, but the last phrase snagged Esther's attention. "Yes. That."

"If the door was locked, then either we missed a really quite large hole in the wall or there was an impressive piece of practice going on," Stephen said. "You look at that, and I'll chase up the loose ends among the China hands?"

Esther tipped her head to one side with what Crane was coming to recognise as her considering look. "Fine. Back at the surgery in a couple of hours?"

"Good. Lord Crane, will you walk with me?"

"Certainly." Crane glanced at Esther. "I've no objection to snouting out anyone else with a grudge against Rackham for you. I just don't propose to drag in someone that I know not to be involved."

"Protecting the lady's name?"

"I didn't say it was a lady."

"No. In fact, you didn't use any pronouns at all," said Esther. "Which does suggest you were avoiding them because they'd be revealing. See you later, Steph."

CHAPTER TEN

They headed out, down Cable Street, in silence for a few hundred yards, until Stephen let out a very long, shuddering breath. "Hell, hell, *hellfire*."

"Don't panic. It's fine."

"No, it isn't!"

"Yes, it is," Crane insisted. "Mrs. Gold knows everything she needs to know about Rackham. You're not hiding anything relevant. I will gladly serve up anyone else Rackham was blackmailing on a plate. Just keep your head."

"Keep my— Do you realise what I said in there?"

"What?"

Stephen clutched at his hair. "I began to tell Esther you're resistant to fluence and had to invent a load of rubbish to cover that up."

"Why should she not know that?"

"Because," said Stephen, with tenuous patience, "the Pied Piper is likely to be someone with latent or undetected talent. Someone with innate resistance to fluence would be exactly the sort of person we're after. Given the way you're tangled up in the middle of this web, she'd be mad not to look at you. And the closer Esther looks at you, the more likely she is to find out about you, and the more likely she is to find out about me. Damn it!"

"No harm done." Crane wasn't entirely sure that was true.

"Esther is not a stupid woman. She knows you're hiding something."

"That's my problem, Stephen."

"No, it really isn't." Stephen had led them down to the river with rapid strides. They paused now, looking across the broad sweep of the churning brown Thames. "Lucien, do you know what I have? In life?"

"What?"

"My profession. That's it. I've no family, except my aunt, and she'll never speak to me again. I live on the pittance they pay justiciars. My friends are all justiciars, or married to them. Everyone else hates us. If I couldn't be a justiciar, I… God, I don't know what I'd do. If I lost that, I'd have lost everything."

"I'm here," Crane observed, without inflection.

Stephen propped his elbows on a bit of wooden fencing. Crane joined him, and they both stared out at the turbid waters.

"You're going back to Shanghai," Stephen said at last.

"What? I'm not."

"Yes, you are, one day. I'm not an idiot, Lucien. You're bored. You had this wonderful life of adventure and excitement and living the way you wanted, and now you're here, no ties, nothing to do, supposed to be in the House of Lords or making a suitable marriage, having to hide how you are, how we are— No, let me finish. I'm not complaining. I…like you, I like spending time with you, but you're not going to tolerate this life forever, or even for much longer. Why would you? I wouldn't stop being a justiciar. And that's the point. You have your life in China, and I have my profession. So I have to make sure I don't lose that profession, and my friends, over this. Over you. I don't want it to come to a choice, but if it does, then I have to choose with the rest of my life in mind."

Crane stared out at the churning waters. A breeze brought a tang of salty air to his nose. He felt oddly calm, but with an unpleasant quivery sensation in his stomach.

He wanted to pull Stephen into his arms, hold him, kiss the fear and the loneliness away, and then fuck him till he forgot any ideas he might have of ending things between them. But he couldn't even touch him, because of the bloody laws of this bloody country that, yes, bored and irritated him beyond bearing.

Could he really say he wouldn't leave, one day?

It didn't matter if he said it or didn't. It would have to be Stephen's choice.

He took a breath, kept his voice level. "I understand. And I've no desire to see you hurt. What do you want me to do?"

"Perhaps we shouldn't…be together. For a while. Till this is over and Esther stops wondering about you and watching me."

Crane looked at his hands, long fingers entwined, so close to Stephen's on the salt-crusted rotting wood, so far from being able to touch him. "If you insist. If you think it would help."

"It might."

Crane nodded slowly. Stephen glanced at him, gnawing his lip. "I'm sorry. I realise this is tiresome. But Rackham's death, and you in the middle of it, and Esther—it's too much, too dangerous. My fault, for bringing you in, but I needed someone who spoke Chinese and could talk to shamans, and I don't think there's anyone in London who fits that bill except you and Rackham, and I had no idea how far this would run out of control." He gave a little involuntary gasp. "I know what it's like to lose everything, you see. I don't want to do that again."

"You won't. Not through my agency. Not at all." Crane hesitated, but it needed saying. "Do you not think that you should talk to Mrs. Gold?"

"About—"

"All of it."

"No."

"She might understand. She might even not be as surprised as you might think."

"No. I can't, Lucien. I can't risk it. It wouldn't be safe."

"Because you don't trust her to know about the power, about me?"

"Exactly."

"Liar," said Crane. Esther Gold's fierce rectitude burned as brightly as Stephen's. He could well understand how the pair of them were so disliked by less upright citizens. There was no doubting Stephen's desire to keep the Magpie Lord's power a secret, but Crane would have put serious money on his lover's trust in Mrs. Gold, and on that trust being well placed. "Try again."

Stephen was silent for a long moment, looking out over the Thames. When he spoke, he addressed the words outwards, as if continuing an argument with the river waters. "You see, my friends aren't all people who've lived in China where nobody cares who you share your bed with. My friends live here, where it matters, where it tells people what kind of man you are. And I don't want them to know that."

"God's sake, Stephen. They're your best friends. This is your *life*."

"It's my life, and my decision," Stephen said sharply. "And until I have a damned good reason to make that decision—"

Being forced apart? Isn't that a good reason? Crane pressed his lips together. Clearly, it wasn't. Stephen wasn't going to gamble with his closest friendships for the sake of a lover he didn't believe would stay around. It made sense.

Stephen's shoulders dropped slightly and he sighed. "It must be nice to be able to talk to your friends."

Crane accepted the change of tone. "Mmm. Leo Hart guessed about you."

"She's never met me!"

"Not you personally. That you exist. That there is someone, for me." *Is? Was?* He didn't want to think about that. "She wants to meet you."

"Um—"

"I said no, don't worry." Crane rolled his shoulders, aching from the stooping position that brought his mouth close to Stephen's ear. "She's the other victim."

"The other... Rackham? He was blackmailing Mrs. Hart?"

"He was, the little turd. That was why I went round to have it out with violence."

"I have to ask," Stephen began.

"I have no reason to believe she knows anything about any of this. I'm quite sure she doesn't. And if she wanted Rackham dead..."

"Yes?"

"Oh, if she wanted him dead, she'd have asked me to kill him," Crane said lightly, recalling that she had done precisely that. "I'll go and tell her the news now. Did you need anything from me regarding the Traders?"

"Not really." Stephen straightened up, indicating that they should walk again. "Dr. Almont is very dull, isn't he? He was so happy to have an audience for his theory on the Javanese *anitu*, or migratory possessive spirit." He mimicked Almont's precise tones. "But he had nothing at all to say on rat cults so I'll spare myself a further lecture."

"Wise," said Crane, as they headed westward, towards town. "What did Peyton say to you?"

"Peyton. Medium height, fifties?"

Crane would have described Peyton as a runt, but since the man stood a good five inches taller than Stephen, he refrained. "And a face like a weasel eating unripe gooseberries."

"Him," said Stephen reflectively. "Yes. He followed me down to the conveniences and told me some rather bad things about you."

"Did he. What sort of things?"

"Apparently, you like to bed men. I was shocked by that, I can tell you."

Crane grinned. "My secret is out. What else?"

Stephen flicked a glance up at him. "He was rather uncomplimentary about Mr. Hart. He had some strong words about Mr. Hart's business dealings, and you for supporting him in them."

"Tom was a thoroughgoing rascal, no denying it. I smuggled for him, and on my own account. I told you that."

"Mmm." Stephen paced on. "He called him a murderer."

"Did he."

"That's not news to you," Stephen observed.

"Tom had men killed," Crane said. "Whether you'd say *murder*—well, we differ on that."

"We do. For example, in my view, if you kill someone for reasons other than self-defence or preventing acts of evil..."

"Yes, very virtuous, but you're not in China."

"Morality is different there?"

"You bloody know it is." Crane saw Stephen blink. "And life is cheaper. Especially in the disreputable quarters of Shanghai. But if that spiteful little worm led you to believe that Tom Hart was some kind of criminal mastermind, or that he and I went around murdering willy-nilly, he's a damned liar."

"There I'll agree with you," Stephen said. "He reeked of malice. Dr. Almont was lethally dull, that man Shaycott managed to make a story about giant rats boring even under current circumstances, and on the whole, I cannot believe you made me put on a fancy suit for that experience."

"It would have been more interesting if you were badly dressed?" Crane asked, striving for his usual tone.

"I'd have felt less like a silk purse in a pig's ear," Stephen retorted.

They bickered amicably back to Ratcliffe Highway, both forcing a lightness neither felt, and if that meant skating over blood and fear and the prospect of parting, Crane was happy with that, but the nauseated feeling in the pit of his stomach was still there when they parted in Oxford Street and he headed westwards to call on Leonora.

CHAPTER ELEVEN

"I'm glad you came." Leonora spoke in Shanghainese, locking the parlour door and putting the key on a side table. She looked drawn, older, obviously lacking sleep. "That bloody worm Rackham was supposed to call and collect five hundred from me today. He hasn't turned up. I keep thinking he's gone to Eadweard. You don't think—"

"I'm sure he hasn't," Crane said. "Leo, what do you want me to do about him?"

"I don't know. Could you not—well, couldn't Merrick do something? What did he do to that horrible tax collector?"

"Broke both his arms and threw him into a high-sided hog pen." Crane had no trouble remembering that incident. "And then stood there watching. I had to help him out in the end, I swear Merrick would have let the pigs eat him. It made the point, though, and we had no more trouble."

"Are there any hog farms in London?" asked Leonora wistfully.

"There are doubtless alternatives. Is that what you want?"

"I don't want to pay blood money for the rest of my life." Leonora's jaw firmed. "I will not let him keep me in fear, either. I don't deserve that." She paused, then added self-mockingly, "I just don't know how to prevent it."

"I wouldn't worry," said Crane. "The little shit's dead."

"He's *what?*" The shock on her face looked genuine. She leapt out of her chair and took a few paces. "Oh God. Lucien, this isn't Shanghai. You have to be careful. What happened? Why?"

"I have no idea. I went round to his rooms and found him dead."

"Oh!" Leonora put a hand to her mouth and let out a relieved sigh. "Oh, thank God. I thought you'd killed him."

"I realise that. Thank you for your good opinion."

"Well, really—" Leonora looked round sharply at a rustle from the walls. "My damned cousins. They do eavesdrop, the nosy bitches. Avoid names. So what happened to him? Did he overdo the opium?"

"No, he was murdered." Crane saw Leo's eyes widen. "Just not by me."

"By whom, then?"

"Presumably someone else he was blackmailing." Crane looked round in his turn at a rattling, scratching sound. "I don't know about eavesdroppers but you definitely have mice."

"How horrid," said Leonora, who had once killed a cobra with her bare hands. "Are you serious, though? He's dead? Oh God, that's…wonderful. That's marvellous! Thank heavens."

"Thank a killer. It wasn't terribly pretty, Leo."

"Oh. No, I suppose not. Well, I'm sorry— No, I'm not. I can't pretend to be. I think really we have to consider it something of a stroke of luck, don't you? Eurgh." Her noise of disgust was directed, not at Rackham's demise, but at the wall. "Listen. The damned things are scuttling up and down all along the other side of the skirting board. How filthy. And I don't even think it's mice," she added, with distaste. "It sounds more like rats."

"Rats," Crane repeated, and the hairs all over his neck and arms rose up in response to the wave of fear. He rubbed his thumb and finger together gently, as Stephen did, and felt—imagined? Felt?—a strange greasiness in the air.

"—because it really isn't. Lucien, are you listening to me?"

"We have to go." Crane turned his head, watching the walls. "Now. Out."

"What? Why?"

"Rats."

"Darling, they'll hardly come in," said Leonora with amusement, and stared at him as he grabbed her arm. "What on earth are you—" Her gaze flitted beyond him and she gave a squawk. "Oh, disgusting!"

Crane turned and saw the rats coming out of the wall.

They looked like the usual vermin, grey-brown, matted, pink-clawed, but they were fighting their way out of a crack in the skirting, not with the desperation he'd seen in rats fleeing a fire, but with a mad aggression that brought the word *rabid* to mind. The first tumbled through into the room with another rat's nose butting hard against its bare fleshy tail, and as it found its feet it looked up at the two horrified humans, and opened its mouth in a yellow-toothed hiss.

Crane lunged for a fire iron. "Unlock the door. Now!"

"But it's just a *fucking hell*!" said Leonora, as the rat grew. It swelled visibly in front of them, eyes bulging black, claws convulsing, huge incisors gnawing the air. Leonora made a high keening sound in her throat as the rat's muscles bulged and inflated under the scabious skin. She bolted to grab the key from the side table, even as Crane brought the poker down hard on the rat's deforming, bubbling skull. It hit the floor at the second the key did, slipping out of Leonora's shaking hands, but that meant nothing, because there were five more of the creatures in the room now, each growing monstrously large, terrifyingly fast.

"Open it, Leo!" Crane caught the second rat in the jaws with the poker as it sprang, and brought the iron down on the third rat's spine as it leapt past him towards Leonora, but that wasn't enough or anything like it to stem the relentless tide. There were more of the things pouring into the room, all lunging towards Leo, two on her now, teeth and claws ripping and scrabbling at her dress as she struggled with the key in the lock. Crane slammed the poker down on a monster's head until he felt bone give, grabbed another rat two-handed and hauled it off the heap of squirming animals, flinging it away. It rebounded off a table, which crashed to the floor taking a bowl of flowers with it, and leapt straight back at Leonora.

Stephen, Stephen, where are you when I need you?

Leonora was screaming, blood blooming through her muslin dress, as she wrenched the door open. A rat landed on her back. She shrieked, fighting her way forward, and Crane waded into the stinking furry mass and pushed at the door, almost closing it on her as she crawled out. He pinned another of the monstrous creatures against the doorframe with his foot to stop it following Leo and, as she disappeared through the gap, slammed the door on it repeatedly till the foul thing went limp.

His back to the door, he was confronted with fifteen or so dog-sized rats. They looked at him with bulging, mad eyes, unmoving, and Crane stared at them with a strange fatalistic calm, which turned to absolute astonishment as they all simultaneously turned and rushed back to their tiny hole of entry in the skirting board, shrinking as fast as they had grown.

It took him half a second to register that he wasn't going to be torn to pieces, and then he realised there was a terrible noise on the other side of the door.

Crane jerked it open to reveal Leonora's two cousins, her aunt and three servants, all shrieking with useless fear. Leonora was on the floor, desperately struggling with the rat on top of her, trying to force its yellow incisors back as it bit at her neck. He grabbed the thing by tail and haunches, pulled it off her bodily, and, for want of a weapon, swung it brutally down against the floor with his full strength, again and again, till something inside it broke.

He dropped the carcass. His ears were ringing. Or, no: everyone was screaming.

Leonora was bleeding freely from neck, shoulders and arms, her dress and flesh torn, making a dreadful sucking noise in her throat. Crane knelt by her. "Leo? Leo, talk to me!"

Her eyes were wide and blind with panic, and she grabbed for him with bloody hands, her grip tightening convulsively as a terrible shudder ran through her body.

"Someone should send for Dr. Grace," quavered Leonora's aunt inadequately, as the stunned group of onlookers clutched each other and made horrified noises.

"I'll take her to a doctor." Crane scooped her up. "Get everyone out of the house. Now." He didn't hear footsteps as he ran down the hall, so he yelled over his shoulder, "There may be more rats!" and heard the panicked cries as he wrenched the front door open and tumbled out into the street.

There was a hansom just a few yards away. He shouted at the jarvey. The man looked round, his eyes widened at the sight of the torn and bleeding woman, and he raised his whip to urge the horse on, but a flurry of magpies rose from the railings and took off past him, chattering wildly, their wings skimming his face as they swooped by. The jarvey recoiled in alarm, and by the time the birds had disappeared, Crane had the carriage door open and was hauling Leo in.

It still cost him valuable seconds of argument and a ludicrous ten pounds to make the jarvey take them to Devonshire Street. The man at least whipped on his horse with alacrity, but even so the ten-minute journey seemed longer than the nights Crane had once spent in a condemned cell waiting for execution. Leonora lay still at first, but as the cab passed up through Piccadilly she began to twitch violently, and she was thrashing around so hard he could barely hold her when the cab jolted to a halt.

"Dr. Gold's surgery," said the cabman, yanking open the door. "And—oh my Gawd."

Crane looked down at Leo in the daylight and swore with spectacular foulness. Her face was, unmistakeably, hideously, swelling, like a bladder inflating under her skin. Her lips were drawn back over teeth that looked very large and very yellow.

Crane dragged her out of the cab, the jarvey's obscenities ringing in his ears, and stumbled up the steps to the door, where, for want of a free hand, he kicked the door violently until an affronted-looking nurse opened it.

"Dr. Gold," he gasped, but she was already calling, "*Doctor!*"

A dark, curly-haired man stuck his head out into the hall. "What's the pr— Great Scott! Bring her in here. Quick, man, on the couch."

Crane put his bloody, convulsing burden on the consulting room couch. Dr. Gold told the nurse, "Hot water, now," grabbing for cloths to stanch the bleeding. "What happened to her?"

"Rats. Giant rats. The ones your wife—"

"Hold her." Dr. Gold stepped away from Leonora, took two steps to the door and bellowed, "Esther? *Esther!*" He hurried back to the couch as the nurse brought hot water in, and shooed her away. "Right, you know about my wife's job? Fine, makes life easier." He spread his hands over Leonora, and Crane saw his eyes darken as his pupils expanded. "What's your name? Hers?"

"Crane. She's Leonora Hart."

"How long ago did this happen?"

"Fifteen minutes— Oh, thank Christ," Crane said, almost folding at the knees, as Esther sprinted in, followed by Stephen. Esther went straight to her husband's side, but Stephen stopped short, eyes widening with horror. "It's Leo," Crane told him. "The rats. The bloody rats got her."

"Hell's teeth," said Esther. "What happened?"

"Are you all right?" Stephen demanded hoarsely.

"Fine." Crane couldn't understand why he was asking, until he glanced down at himself and realised that his shirt and trousers were dark with blood. "I'm fine. They didn't touch me. Not even a scratch. They were trying to kill Leo."

"Still—trying," said Dr. Gold through his teeth.

Stephen and Crane both turned. Dr. Gold stood by Leonora's head, gripping her skull, pupils hugely distended, knuckles white. Esther held his shoulder. He was perspiring. "Can't do this—"

Stephen turned and reached out a hand towards him, and Dr. Gold took a deep shuddering breath. Crane could feel the suction in the air as the three practitioners dragged power towards themselves. Dr. Gold's jaw was set and grim. Leonora jerked violently on the couch, and one clenching, crooked hand flew up in a clawing gesture.

"What's happening?" Esther snapped.

"Can't…stop it. Poison. Bloodstream. Everywhere. Too much. Hold her *down*," said the doctor as Leonora's arms suddenly flailed. Stephen leapt to one side of the couch, Crane to the other, and they each grabbed one of her wrists. Crane gritted his teeth as he struggled to keep her still, unable to believe he wasn't hurting her.

Leonora's cheeks and neck were swelling and shrinking, and her nose and top lip were horribly mobile, sniffing, questing.

"*Anitu*," said Stephen. "Migratory possessive spirit. Is there someone in there, Dan?"

"Don't know. Poison. She's too weak for this. I can't stop it."

Crane stared up at him. He had heard so much from Stephen about Daniel Gold's skills as a healer. He had not allowed himself to think the man could fail.

"Keep trying," he snarled.

"I am. Steph, *more*."

Stephen's hands tightened on Leonora's arm. That was all Crane allowed himself to see, then he concentrated his gaze on his own hands.

If he looked at Stephen now, he knew what his lover would read in his face. He wanted to beg, to plead, to command Stephen to use the Magpie Lord's power, right now, and save Leonora.

But he couldn't do that. Couldn't ask. He had no right. Stephen's life and future depended on the secrets he had to keep. Crane couldn't make that decision for him.

If Stephen kept his secrets, Leonora would die.

Paralysed, Stephen's life and Leonora's death on either side of the scale, throat thick with inexpressible rage and pain, Crane didn't look up when Stephen said his name quietly, or when he repeated it louder. He did look up when Stephen said, "For God's sake!" but it was too late, because Stephen had already reached over, and the scalpel he held seared across the back of Crane's hand, opening a long cut. As Crane's eyes flew to his face, Stephen sliced open the heel of his own hand, reached over Leo's thrashing body again and slapped his bloody wound onto Crane's.

"Steph!" shrieked Esther, with absolute horror.

"Hold on tight, Dan," said Stephen calmly. His eyes met Crane's for just a second, wide and strained with something that didn't show in his voice, and then he drew on the power, the tingling in his hands turning to needles of hot ice that stabbed through Crane's skin, and suddenly Stephen's eyes were full of magpies.

Crane felt it like a wave, cresting through his body, a rush of goose pimples through muscle and organs and bone. The hair prickled on his head, and stood up visibly on Stephen's, as his eyes flashed black, white and blue. Stephen pulled harder, lifting Crane higher, an almost orgasmic feeling of exquisite tension running through him. Esther was shouting and Leonora was wailing and Dr. Gold was grunting with agony or pleasure as Stephen lit the power in Crane's blood into spectacular, glorious life—

—and they reached the top.

Crane blinked. He felt a strange, calm, slightly dizzy sensation, not unlike a mild opium buzz, a sense of dissociation, as though he would have to move carefully to be sure his mind didn't leave his body behind.

Stephen's eyes were blazing gold around huge pupils, black and white shadows fluttering and flickering. His face was very still.

Dr. Gold, by contrast, was wearing an incredulous grin.

"Oh, yes." He swept his hands over Leonora, and the horrible thrashing stopped. "*Oh*, yes. Oh, this is beautiful. Let's get you out, shall we?"

"What the devil do you think you're doing?" His wife's voice was shrill.

"My job, my love." Dr. Gold smiled beatifically.

Esther turned and stalked away, arms folded, face red.

"Out you come now. Oh, this is easy, so very easy." Dr. Gold moved a hand like a conductor and a thick brownish smoke erupted from Leonora's wounds, eyes and mouth, pouring into the air and evaporating on the instant. "Out, out, out, *gone*. There. Dear me, what was all the fuss about? And now, let's fix this lady up." He looked down at Leonora's face and put both hands over it. One deep breath, then his head snapped back, mouth open ecstatically. The air around his hands was thick and viscous.

Crane glanced at Stephen, who was looking down at Leonora, face unreadable. His hand lay on Crane's, over her body. He was wearing the Magpie Lord's ring on his finger. Usually he kept it on a chain round his neck, to avoid the ancient carved gold attracting attention. It was too late for that now.

"Keep your hands clear, Mr. Crane," Dr. Gold said. "Here it comes."

It was, simply, healing. Down from her shoulder, the flesh knitted and mended as Crane watched with numb acceptance, the tears and bites repairing themselves. Leo's sick pallor changed to a healthier pink, her breathing became steady and gentle, and finally Dr. Gold lifted his hands from her head and looked down at unmarked skin, with only the slightest fading lines to show where the horrible tears had been.

"*Tsaena*," Crane whispered. "Thank you, Doctor."

"Don't thank him," Esther said. "It's not his power."

The doctor looked up, eyes very bright. "But I can use it. Oh, I can use it. Mrs. Henville's cancer. Lucy Gillett's consumption—"

"No, no, no, *no*." Esther's voice was harsh. "Stop this."

"But look at what I can do. Think who I can heal. So many people." His face was alight with wild wonder and greed.

"Stop this, Danny. Stop it now."

"Don't. I don't want it to stop."

"*Stop it!*"

Stephen jerked his hand violently away from Crane's, and the world snapped back to normality with a disorienting jolt, like the sensation of falling in a dream. Dr. Gold gave a cry of pain and rage, and reached a hand towards Crane, but Esther was right in his face now, talking urgently. Stephen span away and stood, facing the wall. Crane looked down at Leonora, unmarked and peaceful, at his own hand that showed no trace of a wound, at his lover's tense, hunched shoulders, then over at the Golds. Dr. Gold was sitting on a stool at the head of the couch now, face in his hands, Esther holding him with angry care.

As the power drained out of the room, the silence grew.

"So," Esther said finally. "Blood magic."

"It wasn't—" began Stephen, without looking round.

"You used his blood. You've been using his blood for months."

"Twice. I've done it twice. And it *wasn't*—"

"Don't lie to me." Esther's voice cut like a whip. "I've seen you riding this. What are you doing, cutting him? Drinking it?" Her tone was thick with anger and contempt.

"I haven't done anything like that." Stephen's voice was flat and hopeless. "That was the second time. If you don't believe me—"

"No, I don't believe you!" Esther screamed. "I *saw* you. That's the power you've been drawing on for *months* and I stood up for you in front of the Council and told them, no, Stephen Day is not turning warlock, and now *this*—blood magic right in front of me, and you don't even have the spine to look me in the face and admit it, you cowardly little—"

"*Mrs. Gold!*" roared Crane, in a voice trained by ten years on a trading floor. It rang off the walls, jolted Dr. Gold into looking up, and momentarily silenced Esther.

"Mrs. Gold," Crane repeated, with slightly less volume. "Mr. Day told you the absolute truth. That was the second time he's used my blood in that way, and the first time was to save my life. This business is none of his choosing or his seeking, it's my fault if it's anyone's, and if you need to shout at someone, Mrs. Gold, then you can shout at me and we'll see who shouts loudest."

"I don't want to shout," Esther said through her teeth, addressing the words to Stephen. "I want an explanation. You're telling me it's not blood magic. Very well, let's say that's true. Then how the devil have you been riding that power for months? If you've not been using blood magic, *what's the source?*"

Stephen turned then. He was chalk white. "It's, um—it is a transference, but the blood is purely catalytic. You can see that. If I'd stripped that power out of him, he'd be a heap of dust."

"That's true, Esther," said Dr. Gold wearily. "I really would have noticed."

"A catalyst. And his blood has *been* a catalyst for the last few months because—?"

"It hasn't. Well, not, not precisely. It, um, I—"

Esther folded her arms. Her face was disbelieving, and disgusted.

"Look." Stephen shut his eyes. "It's, um…well, it is physical, only not blood, but it happens when, when we—" His voice dried up, and he flung a desperate look at Crane, who took two strides forward at that mute appeal, unclenching his fists from the white-knuckled nail-in-palm position that he had used to make himself keep silent, and put both hands possessively on Stephen's slender, shaking shoulders.

"*Oh*," said Dr. Gold.

"Stephen and I are lovers." Crane held Esther's eyes as they widened. He didn't want her to look at Stephen. "Have been for some four months. That is what causes the transfer of power, as I understand it. No blood magic, no warlockry. It happens when we go to bed, it's something to do with my family line, it's not within my control or his. That's the long and short of it, and if you have any opinions to offer on the matter, you can address them to me." More aggression than he'd intended rang in the last words, but he was damned if Stephen would stand here and take abuse.

Esther stared back at him, face tight. Crane saw Dr. Gold's intent form at the corner of his eye. Under his hands, Stephen was rigid with tension, head bowed.

"Is this true?" Esther said at last.

"Yes. He—we— Yes."

"You and he. And he's a source."

"Blood, bone and birdspit." Stephen's voice was thin. "You can't tell anyone, either of you, not about him being a source. Please. Say what you need to the Council, Esther, tell them anything, I'll resign of course, but we can't let people know about this. They'll tear him apart."

"You are not resigning on my account," Crane said harshly. "He has not put a foot out of line, Mrs. Gold. He has not done a damned thing wrong."

Stephen gave an almost-laugh. "Lucien, we're breaking the *law*."

Esther was looking at Stephen. "And this is why you've been letting us think you've gone bad. To hide this. For pity's sake!" She turned abruptly away. Stephen twitched violently, and Crane gripped him tighter.

Dr. Gold let out a long sigh. "Oh, Steph. You might have said something."

Stephen made a strangled noise. Crane drawled, "Might he?"

"Yes, actually, he might. We're not imbeciles. Great Scott, man, did it not occur to you we'd understand?"

"I don't understand," said Esther, swinging back round. Her face was red. "You swine, Stephen Day. You *pig*. You horrible, vile—I thought—God damn you, I was so frightened!"

Her voice broke. Crane felt Stephen's body stiffen under his hands. He instinctively clenched his fingers on his lover's shoulders, but Stephen twisted free with a hoarse, "Es!", and bolted towards his partner.

Esther flung herself into his arms and wept, choking with angry sobs. Stephen muttered something incoherent, face pressed into her shoulder, and Esther thumped him on the back with a hard fist. "Why didn't you say?" she managed through her tears. "Why didn't you just *say*?"

Crane took a step back from the pair, almost light-headed with relief, and heard a low whistle from the couch. He turned to see Dr. Gold jerking his head in summons, and moved over to him. "Doctor?"

"Nothing, really," said Dr. Gold quietly. "It's just that if Esther realises you've seen her cry, she'll never forgive you."

"Ah. Thank you." Crane turned from Stephen and Esther, who were now talking tearfully, urgently and simultaneously. He could hear Stephen repeating, "I'm sorry, I'm sorry," and Esther's furious, "I don't *care* about that!"

He concentrated on Dr. Gold instead. "Are you all right, Doctor?"

Dr. Gold made a face. He looked rather worn. "I've had worse. So. You and Stephen."

"Yes. You don't seem surprised."

"Well, he's been my best friend for ten years and my wife's partner for five. We have had occasion to observe him. It's the total lack of interest in the fair sex that gives it away, over the long run," Dr. Gold added helpfully.

"I'll make a note."

"This business with the power started when he came back from that rather dramatic trip to the country in spring," Dr. Gold said. "Which I seem to recall he said was a blood, bone and birdspit job. Now, does that make you the chap whose ancestor was the Magpie Lord?"

"It does, yes. Lord Crane." He held his hand out.

Dr. Gold shook it. "Daniel Gold. Well, I can see why Steph's been keeping you quiet, quite apart from the other. I am right in thinking it was your father who hounded Steph's father to death?"

That was blunt, not to say brutal. Crane kept his voice level. "It was, yes."

"Mmm. Hardly an auspicious start, I'd have thought."

It hadn't been remotely auspicious. Crane's hated family had cast a very dark shadow over his first encounters with Stephen. He didn't intend to discuss that, so he simply shrugged.

Dr. Gold cocked an eyebrow. "One might wonder why Steph would enter into a, er, liaison under such unpromising circumstances."

"You'd need to speak to him about it."

"I'll do that, the next time I want to hear a pack of bare-faced lies. Lord Crane, I know Steph extremely well. And this is the first time I've known him risk arrest, disaster and the destruction of his professional reputation. Consider me fascinated that he's doing so on your account. Fascinated, and just a little concerned."

"I don't intend to let him suffer any consequences."

"I very much doubt you can avert them, in the long run," Dr. Gold said. "This strikes me as something of a dangerous game."

Crane checked quickly over his shoulder to be sure the two justiciars were still intent on one another. "I understand your concern, Doctor. Notwithstanding which, and with the greatest respect, it's none of your business."

Dr. Gold opened his hands, apparently unoffended. "Perhaps not. Although he's weeping over my wife in my surgery. That surely gives me some say in the matter, if only to ask him to take it somewhere else."

Crane wasn't sure how to answer that, so he didn't. The doctor continued, "We're fond of Steph, you know. Despite appearances. I don't wish to see him hurt."

"I trust Mrs. Gold feels the same."

Dr. Gold made a face. "Esther's bark is worse than her bite. Well, actually, it isn't, but she's entitled to do some barking anyway. Steph's put her through a miserable few months with all this."

"It hasn't been very entertaining for him either," Crane returned swiftly, and saw a glint of something like approval in Dr. Gold's expression.

"Well, as you say, it's his business. But watch your step, Lord Crane. And perhaps bear in mind that you may consult me in confidence, professionally speaking." Crane had no idea what that was supposed to mean, but Dr. Gold looked past him before he could ask. "Ah, the march of justice. Have you two finished?"

Crane turned to see that Esther and Stephen had come up behind him, both somewhat red of cheek and eye, but under more control. He flicked an eyebrow at Stephen and received a quick, watery smile.

"Er. Dan…" Stephen began awkwardly.

Dr. Gold gripped Stephen's shoulder and gave it a slight shake. "Stephen Day, you're a blithering idiot."

"I know."

"Good," Esther said. "And now that's all sorted out, we have work to do."

CHAPTER TWELVE

Before any work could be done, Dr. Gold had to wake Leonora from her magically induced unconsciousness. He began a careful explanation, as she stared at her unbitten arms, which Crane interrupted with a brisk, "They're shamans. It was magic."

Leonora accepted the situation fairly rapidly, under the circumstances, but declined to be interviewed in the bloody rags of her gown, so Esther took her off to borrow a dress, and Dr. Gold disappeared to find Crane a shirt, while they waited for Merrick, who had been summoned to bring replacements for his gory clothing.

That left Stephen and Crane briefly alone.

"Are you all right?" Crane asked.

Stephen walked over and held on to as much of Crane as he could reach, burying his face in the stained shirtfront, gripping tight. "Oh God, Lucien. God. I was so frightened."

"I know. You looked a great deal less scared when we were about to be murdered by warlocks."

"That was only death. This was Esther." Stephen snuggled closer, rubbing his face on Crane's chest, trembling slightly. "Oh God, I'm such a coward. Don't let me go."

"I don't intend to," Crane said, caressing the curly hair, and something rang in his voice that made Stephen look up.

"You didn't ask me to do it." He pulled away slightly. "You don't owe me anything. It was my choice."

Crane heard the words from long ago that morning: *I have to choose with the rest of my life in mind.* His hands tightened on the smaller man, pulling him back, as close as he could come.

"You know, Gold's right. You're a fool, and I'm another. Between us, we'd barely make a village idiot. God damn the man," he added as footsteps sounded, coming down the stairs. "I *will* talk to you later."

"What does that mean?" said Stephen warily.

"Shout at. Fuck. Adore. Come here." He pulled Stephen's chin up and planted a hard kiss on his mouth, then let him go just as Dr. Gold banged the door open, with a smock-like linen shirt in his hand.

"All I've got that might fit you, I'm afraid, here you go. The ladies are ready. If you go upstairs, I might even be able to see some patients. What the devil is that?"

"Tattoos." Crane finished stripping off his stained shirt as the doctor stared in astonishment at his decorated, animated skin. "I had them done in China."

"They're moving!"

"They do," Stephen said. "Don't ask."

"This is typical of you, Steph," said Dr. Gold bitterly. "Typical. Of course you can't just be unnatural like everyone else. Go on, get this overgrown magic lantern out of my way, this is a surgery, not a circus. Out!"

Leonora and Esther were waiting upstairs in the Golds' small drawing room when Crane walked in, still grinning. It was a small space, with bare floorboards and cheap furniture covered up by cushions and rugs, piles of books, and a couple of rather attractive wall hangings with lettering that Crane guessed to be Hebrew. The two women were sitting together as Crane and Stephen entered. As well as their similar colouring, they were much of a height, though Leonora filled the plain, borrowed gown almost to bursting. Esther didn't give the impression of being aware of the unflattering contrast.

"You look wonderfully…intact," Crane told Leo. "Stephen, Mrs. Hart. Leo, this is Stephen Day. In case you don't know yet, Mrs. Gold and Mr. Day are justiciars. Shamanic law enforcers. Now, pay attention. The rats that attacked you also killed Rackham. Before that, they killed two men in Limehouse, and a family on Ratcliffe Highway. There's probably but not necessarily a shaman behind this. The rats were very definitely trying to kill you; they didn't touch me. So who's after you?"

"Nobody."

"Do better."

"I said, nobody," Leonora snapped. "Nobody is trying to kill me. I have no enemies."

"What about Rackham?"

"What about him? He's dead."

"He was blackmailing you." Crane caught her outraged look. "Don't get your stockings in a knot, *adai*, Mrs. Gold is the only person in this room who he wasn't distinguishing with his attentions. As far as I know."

"No," said Esther firmly. "Mrs. Hart, who else was he blackmailing?"

"I've no idea!"

"The thing is," Stephen said, "you and Rackham clearly have a common enemy. The blackmail is the obvious link—"

"I have had nothing to do with that little toe rag since before Tom died. He was a junk-sick waste of skin." Leonora sounded entirely sincere. "The matter that he was blackmailing me about is not…creditable, perhaps, but I can't see how it's related to anything else. Who are the other dead?"

"The family on Ratcliffe Highway were called Trotter," Stephen said. "The Chinese who died were Tsang Ma and Bo Yi."

"I've never heard of them," said Leonora.

"Well, what about Java?" asked Crane. "Specifically, Sumatra. The Dutch East Indies. That seems to be the source of the rat problem."

"So?"

Crane switched to Shanghainese to say, "Your second husband was Dutch."

"Excuse me," said Esther loudly. "We'll do this in English please."

"That related to a private matter. I don't see any possible connection." Leonora looked from Stephen to Esther. "I'm extremely grateful that you saved my life, but I know absolutely nothing of this. I don't know anything about Sumatra beyond having the same few acquaintances as Lord Crane, I have no idea what Rackham was up to, I've never heard of any of these people. I honestly can't think of any reason why anyone would try to kill me. Could it not have been a mistake? They were trying to kill someone else? It seems more probable."

"So far the rats have been used on two Chinese practitioners, one old China hand and you, back from China," Esther said. "That seems to me to be a pattern."

"What does 'practitioners' mean?" Leonora asked.

Crane opened his mouth to reply, but at that point there was a polite knock, and Merrick came in with a bundle. "I beg your pardon," he began, and then recoiled at his master's appearance. "What happened to you?"

"Blame Leo. She bled all over me."

"That's the Hawkes and Cheney suit!" said Merrick, outraged. "I'll never get that stain out."

"I'll bleed more carefully next time," Leonora assured him. "Hello, Frank."

"Missus. You all right?"

"She's fine. It was the rats." Crane took the parcel. "The ones that got Rackham. While you're here, I don't suppose you know anything about Tsang Ma and Bo Yi?"

Merrick looked blank. "Can't say I do, my lord. Who's that, then?"

"The dead shamans."

"What, the ones the rats killed, down in Limehouse? That's not their names, is it?"

"Yes."

"You sure?" said Merrick, frowning. "Could have sworn they said something else."

"Said?" Stephen repeated. "Weren't they dead?"

"I didn't mean when they was dead, sir," Merrick said kindly. "I mean, back in China."

Crane choked. "What? When?"

"When I bumped into 'em back home. Good few years back, that was."

"*You knew them?* Why the hell didn't you say?"

"Why didn't I say what?" demanded Merrick. "'Hey, them two Chinese shamans, they was shamans from China?' I told you every time I passed someone I ever met, we'd never talk about anything else! My lord."

Crane glared at him. "You're not fooling anyone, you know. So who are they?"

Merrick turned his hands up in exasperation. "I dunno, do I? They was a couple of bumpkin shamans I met in some clapshop. Nobodies. You didn't know them, I didn't know them."

"So why do you remember them?" asked Stephen.

"Well, you don't see shamans in a whorehouse much, sir. And they was a funny-looking pair. Pretty torn up when I saw them the other day, and they'd got old, ain't we all, but one of 'em had this, like, flower shape on his cheek, birthmark sort of thing, and the other one had a face like *ma po do fu*. Very pockmarked, is what I mean, sir. Stuck in the mind."

"Yes, Mrs. Hart?" said Esther.

Everyone else turned. Leonora was staring at nothing, mouth slightly open. Her skin was pallid.

"Leo?" said Crane.

"Who were the shamans, Mrs. Hart?" Esther asked.

"Pa Ma and Lo Tse-fun," Leonora whispered. "They're dead? And so is Rackham… Oh, no. No no no. I have to get out of here."

"You're going nowhere." Crane grasped her wrist as she leapt up.

"Get off me!"

Crane tightened his grip. "Sit down."

Leonora struggled fruitlessly. "Let me go, you bastard," she snarled in English, and slapped a hand over her mouth like a child.

"Watch your language," said Crane. "And stop playing the fool. Whatever this is about, your best chance is to tell these two about it right now."

Leonora swallowed. "They'll want me dead."

"If you tell us who they are, we can stop them," Stephen said.

"No. I mean you. You'll want me dead."

Stephen and Esther looked at each other.

"In the general way," Stephen said carefully, "we don't often want people dead."

"Speak for yourself," said Esther. "Why don't you tell us about it, Mrs. Hart, and let us be the judges of what we think."

"Nobody ain't going to lay a finger on you, missus," said Merrick. "Not while me and my lord are standing. You tell Mr. Day about it and don't worry no more."

"Since when did *you* talk to the law?" demanded Leonora in Shanghainese.

"Since his nobility's been fucking it," Merrick returned. "You want the shortarse on your side."

"That'll do." Crane spoke in English. "Sit, please."

He pulled at Leo's wrist once more, and she collapsed without resistance onto a chair, her eyes bright with unshed tears.

"This is about Tom, isn't it?" said Crane, watching her. "What happened? What did he do?"

"Who's Tom?" Esther asked.

Leonora scrubbed at her face with the heels of her hands. "My husband. He was a…businessman, in Shanghai."

"Tom had a small legitimate trading concern, and a rather larger illegitimate one," Crane said crisply. "He ran a few smuggling operations as well as funding various less-than-reputable businesses. He was pretty ruthless and a bad man to cross. On you go."

"He loved you," Leonora said reproachfully.

"I loved him. What did he do?"

"Pa and Lo. They were shamans. From Xishan, in the countryside. But they didn't want to be shamans, they wanted to be city boys. Do you—is it the same for shamans here?"

"I doubt it." Crane looked at the two justiciars. "Chinese shamans are more like a priesthood, like monks even. There's rigorous training, asceticism, they don't drink or gamble or use drugs. They can marry but they don't whore. They live rightly."

"Well, Pa and Lo weren't like that," Leonora said. "I think they'd run away from Xishan. They wanted to live the life in Shanghai, but they had no money and really, they were a pair of bumpkins, utterly hopeless. And Tom…well, he saw an opportunity."

"To…?"

"To use their skills. That was what Tom did, he got people to do things for him. And here were these two country boys, all they wanted was to go drinking and whoring and gambling without getting taken away for re-education by the other shamans, and they had these astonishing powers. So Tom took them under his wing."

"Hold on." Crane was frowning. "When was this? I don't remember any of this."

"You were in the north that year, playing the fool with that warlord. It started after you'd gone, and ended long before you were back." Leo took a deep breath. "Pa and Lo were stupid and greedy and lazy, but they weren't particularly bad men. Not at first. But something happened to them. Corruption." Her eyes were distant. "They went bad, quickly. They became nasty drunks. They liked their work for Tom too much."

"Doing what?"

"Reminding people to pay their bills. Setting up deals. Solving problems. That sort of thing."

"Shamans did that stuff?" Merrick sounded shocked.

Leonora shrugged impatiently. "You know how Tom was. He kept them supplied with drink and girls and opium and let them gamble in his places, and they did what he needed. I didn't like them. They were just the usual sort at first, but they changed. They began to frighten me, eventually."

"Perhaps Chinese shamans have a reason for their rules," said Esther mildly.

"And then Rackham got in trouble. He was working with them and Tom, as an intermediary of sorts. And he asked for help, and Pa and Lo went, and… The girl died." She bit her lip. "They killed her."

"Shamans?" said Crane. "Shamans killed a girl?"

Leonora nodded, staring at her intertwined hands. "I don't know if they meant to. They said it was an accident. But she was dead. So Tom helped them to…you know."

"Cover it up?" Crane could sense Stephen's eyes on him and felt the unfamiliar, unwelcome prickle of shame.

"But someone found out anyway. Another shaman came to Tom. He knew all about it. He said Pa and Lo would be taken for judgement and Rackham would be handed over for murder. He said Tom would be judged for his part in corrupting them. He was angry and he threatened them and—" She licked her lips. "They panicked. Pa and Lo and Rackham. I suppose he wasn't expecting them to fight, but they did. They killed him."

"Another shaman. While I was in the north." Crane's voice sounded hollow in his own ears, and an awful suspicion was building at the back of his mind.

"He'd come alone. Shamans usually work alone in China," Leonora explained to Esther. "And Rackham said if we put the body in an iron box, and threw it in the harbour, it couldn't be traced. So that's what we did. And—"

"Hang on." The same unwelcome thought had obviously just hit Merrick. "This shaman, missus. You ain't saying—"

"Xan Ji-yin," said Crane. "Tom had Xan Ji-yin killed? *Tom?*"

"He didn't have him killed! It just…happened."

"Mother *fuck*!" Crane leapt up from his seat and stalked over to the window. "I beg your pardon, Mrs. Gold. My apologies."

"Don't mind me," said Esther dryly. "Make amends by telling me who this man was."

Crane put his hands through his hair. "One of the most powerful, influential shamans in Shanghai. His disappearance was still a scandal when we came back from Manchuria. They never stopped looking for him. Imagine knocking the Archbishop of Canterbury on the head and chucking him in the Thames."

Esther whistled, unladylike. "The body wasn't found?"

"Not by the time we left, and that was less than a year ago. This must be what, thirteen years back?"

"But what about those flagpoles? I thought dreadful things happened if you didn't bury shamans properly."

"You said something about their souls becoming vampires." Stephen's voice was professional and unemotional. "That's rather close to this Java business, the *anitu*. Souls of the dead taking animal form for purposes of murder."

"You think it's this Xan chap possessing the rats?" said Esther thoughtfully. "Well, that would be interesting."

"That's not the word," Crane snapped. "Surely to God that's not possible. It was on the other side of the world!"

Esther shrugged. "What did this precious pair, and Rackham, do after murdering the archbishop?"

"Tom got rid of them. He sent Pa and Lo to the other end of China and put Rackham on a ship to Macao, told them all never to come back. I never heard anything about Pa or Lo again. Rackham came back a few years later, after Tom died, with an opium habit." Leonora looked around helplessly. "I thought it was over. I forgot about it."

Crane sat down and put his face in his hands. "You forgot."

"Well, what did you want me to do?" snapped Leonora. "Get the harbour dredged and present his bones to the next of kin? Go to a nunnery? The man's dead!"

"Who's avenging him?" asked Stephen.

Leonora shook her head. "I don't know. He had apprentices, followers. It could be anyone."

"You don't agree?" Stephen asked Crane, watching his face.

"It doesn't feel right. I can't help thinking they'd have come on a lot stronger if it was Xan's followers. Taken Pa and Lo and Rackham back for judgement, confronted you directly. I'd have expected rather more of a performance made of it. This business with the rats is vengeance, not justice. Especially with the Ratcliffe Highway deaths. That's not what shamans—true shamans—would do."

Esther nodded. "What about the girl?"

"Which girl?" asked Leonora blankly.

"The one whose murder your husband concealed," Stephen said. Crane felt himself flinch along with Leonora. "Who was she?"

Leonora reddened. "I wasn't thinking— I don't know who she was. Her name was Arabella. She was with the Baptist mission. I don't know anything else. Tom didn't tell me and I didn't want to know."

"Rackham had an English girl killed?" said Crane incredulously.

"Is that worse than a Chinese girl?" asked Esther.

"Less usual. Was her body dumped too?" Crane asked Leonora.

"I don't know. I suppose so."

"Right," Stephen said. "So we have our link between the rat victims. There remains the possible Java connection—anything coming back to mind on that, Mrs. Hart? No? And other than that, we have two very clear motives of vengeance. We need to know who this Arabella was. Lord Crane, can you assist?" he asked formally.

Everyone in this room knows we're fucking. Please, don't do this. Crane made himself meet Stephen's neutral look with an equally blank one. "I can ask. Cryer will recall a name if anyone does."

"Then you and I will go to Mr. Cryer. Esther and Mr. Merrick will stay with Mrs. Hart for now, in case of rats. Es, whistle up the others please. If the rats come after Mrs. Hart again, keep a couple alive for me, and we will track this back. If not, we'll leave her with Joss, and the rest of us will go chase down any connections or, failing that, turn Limehouse over for friends or relatives of this man Xan."

"You're assuming Lord Crane and Mr. Merrick's cooperation," Esther observed mildly.

"Yes, I am," Stephen said. "You'd better change, Lord Crane."

Esther and Stephen left them in the drawing room. Crane changed his clothes rapidly, knowing Leo didn't care.

"Well, this is a fuck-up," remarked Merrick in Shanghainese, handing him his trousers.

"It is, yes."

"That's him, the little one? Yours?" Leo asked.

"Yes." *I hope.*

"Not your usual type," she observed.

"His usual type is dangerous buggers," Merrick said. "And there's no change there. Do *not* piss Mr. Day about."

"What are they going to do to me?" she asked in a thread of a voice.

"Nothing," Crane said. "You're not in their jurisdiction. Things are different here. Their job is to stop people misusing magic. They might not be very impressed with that story, but unless they find out you personally murdered Xan or the girl, they've nothing to say to you."

"Then why are you scared?" asked Leonora.

Crane pulled on his coat with no respect for its quality. "Let's just get on, shall we?"

CHAPTER THIRTEEN

Crane and Stephen took a hackney to Town's lodgings, which were in the Holborn area, more for private conversation than to save the walk, although no conversation was forthcoming at first. Finally, Crane took a deep breath and started somewhere.

"Are you all right? With the Golds?"

"Maybe. Probably. It depends how Esther feels once she's stopped being happy I'm not a warlock. But, well, I said I'd understand if she wanted a new partner, and she said yes, she wanted one who wasn't congenitally stupid, so I think things might be all right. You can say 'I told you so' if you want."

Crane let out a long breath, feeling one knot of tension ease. "I'm glad."

"I suppose they always knew, really. Dan wasn't surprised, was he?"

"Not at all."

"What were you talking about with him?"

"He was trying to decide if I'm good enough for you." Crane grinned at Stephen's expression. "Not quite in those words, of course."

"He, er, can be a bit blunt sometimes," Stephen said cautiously.

"So can I. It's entirely reasonable, Stephen. He's your friend, he's concerned for you."

"And look what I did to him, what I put him through. I've told you about the craving for power—well, you saw it then. It was a foul thing to do to him without warning."

"He said he's had worse," Crane commented. "And, if I may say so, you had the same thing happen to you out of nowhere four months back, and you haven't been madly craving power ever since, have you?" He paused. "Have you? Shit. Stephen—"

"It's fine."

"No, it isn't. How hard has this been for you?" Crane felt a surge of guilt, another unfamiliar sensation. "Why didn't you tell me?"

"It's nothing I can't manage," Stephen said. "It's hardly as if I've been practising self-denial. Every time we go to bed—"

"But that's on a different scale. *I* know that's different and I'm no practitioner."

Stephen rubbed at his face. "Look, I have three choices. I never see you again so I'm not tempted; I give in to temptation and milk you for power until I'm a raging madman; or I control myself. I don't like the first two options."

"Nor do I." Crane reached for his hand. Stephen's fingers were still humming with power, the familiar needles stabbing Crane's nerves. "I'm sorry. I didn't know. Can I make it easier for you?"

"It's fine. This is my problem, Lucien."

Crane bit back his urge to insist, took a breath, felt his way carefully. "It occurs to me that I have never fully appreciated my good fortune that you were the shaman that came to help me. Not only that I got my hands on your delectable arse, but that apparently most of your colleagues would have turned into power-mad lunatics through my malign influence, whereas you remain the strongest and the best man I know. I'd thank Rackham again for introducing us, were he not dead, and had I not planned to kill him myself." He heard Stephen's snort, felt a wave of relief at an obstacle negotiated. "Why do you think the Chinese shamans went bad?"

Stephen sighed. "We're precariously balanced people, you know. Having too much power drives you mad and so does having too little. Using it too much can be very, very bad; not using it is worse. Perhaps there's something in the system you described, bodily asceticism, self-denial. Maybe that helps them control it. I don't know. We don't act like monks here, the Church doesn't love us, so nobody feels any great urge to ape its ways. Anyway, to answer your question, it sounds like Pa and Lo relied on their physical discipline for mental control. When one went, so did the other."

"And thus they were corrupted. Tom corrupted them," Crane said. "God, I find that deeply disheartening. That Tom could do that."

"It wasn't an inspiring story. But…well, were you really surprised by it?"

"Yes, actually, I was. Not that he covered up murder. He would, if they were his men." Crane caught the other's look. "Oh, please, Stephen, what do you imagine happens to men who die in pub fights or street brawls down in Limehouse? A coroner's inquest and a decent burial?"

"I know that, but—"

"A rival sends a few thugs to your house to break your kneecaps. Pitched battle, two of them get killed. You call the law, get thrown in jail as a matter of course, spend half your fortune on bribes to get out, and the other half on lawyers for the next two years. Or you dump the bodies in the river and have done. It amazes me they can get ships through for the corpses."

Stephen grimaced. "If the law isn't just, I see your point. But that's not what happened here."

"No. It's not. But I'm sure Tom didn't order the killing of a girl who posed no threat, and I don't…I don't want to believe he ordered Xan's death. I prefer to believe it happened as Leo told it." He felt Stephen's fingers tighten. "Tom was a hard man, but he wasn't a bad one. He never corrupted innocents."

"No? How old were you when he turned you into a smuggler?" Stephen asked. "Come to that, how old was Mrs. Hart when he married her?"

"Leo was eighteen when they married, and she'd do it again in a heartbeat. I was nineteen when I started working for him, and as for innocent… I'd been selling my arse for months by then in an effort not to starve. Merrick was getting shit beaten out of him in the fight cages every few days, because a white man was enough of a novelty to bring in a few cash even if he lost. We had the corner of a filthy room in the worst of the slums, living on dishwater congee and cheap *baijiu*, the stuff that can send you blind. We were royally fucked, Stephen. We would not have made it through one more winter. Then we met Tom in a drinking den, we talked, and that evening he paid off our debts and gave us work, money upfront. He hauled us out of the gutter and saved our lives, for no more reason than he thought we might be worth it."

Stephen's fingers were clenched on his, painfully hard, eyes wide and appalled. "You never told me this. You said you were poor, but—I had no idea—"

"Don't look like that, sweet boy. It doesn't matter. It's been over for a very long time. I'm just trying to explain Tom. He wasn't moral, by any standards, but he wasn't a bad man, and I'm surprised that he crossed that line. Corrupting shamans is wrong. Grotesque." Crane searched for words, struggling to convey the visceral revulsion any Shanghai-dweller would feel. "They're better than the rest of us. Encouraging them to drink and whore and dice is like—I don't know, pissing on a church altar." He thought about it. "And Tom would probably have done that too, if he needed a piss and the church was convenient. Oh, maybe I'm not so surprised, after all. He had the devil of a strong personality, it was hard not to be carried away, to make him into more than he was."

"It doesn't sound as though Pa and Lo were particularly unwilling to be carried," Stephen said. "We're all responsible for ourselves. They made their choices to fall, even if Hart helped them down. And they were shamans, after all. Not powerless."

"Maybe. But you could follow Tom to hell and not notice where you were going till your shoes caught fire."

"Charm's a very dangerous thing. Lucien, tell me," Stephen said thoughtfully. "This respect for shamans, this inviolability…"

"Mmm?"

"Well, I don't know if you remember, but some three weeks ago you tied me to your bedposts and spent two hours subjecting me to acts of unimaginable depravity. And considering you call me a shaman—"

"I take issue with 'unimaginable'," Crane interrupted, sudden heat and light rushing through him. "I imagine those acts in detail every night you're not there. In fact, I've imagined quite a few more that I have every intention of subjecting you to when I get a chance."

"Really?" murmured Stephen, shifting closer. "Like what?"

"That's for me to know and you to find out when you're chained to my bed. And I do mean chained. With iron, next time. I want you helpless." He felt Stephen's quiver over the motion of the carriage. "Naked, helpless, pleading. And absolutely vulnerable to everything I choose to do to you."

Stephen gulped. "You do love to put me on my knees, don't you?"

"I like to make you know your master," Crane said. "It's only fair. The rest of the time, you've got me so thoroughly enslaved, I might as well be wearing a collar with your name on it."

"What? Lucien— Oh, God *damn* it!" Stephen said, as the hackney jolted to a stop.

Crane hissed, trying to force down his arousal. "I swear, we will have a proper conversation at some point today if I have to do murder to make it happen. We couldn't just go home, I suppose?"

"Come on." Stephen hopped out of the carriage. "Let's get this over."

They caught Town as he was on his way out of his lodgings for luncheon. Crane was startled to realise it was not quite noon. The day seemed to have gone on forever.

"Good to see you, dear chap," Town told Crane. "And Mr. Day, nice to meet you again. Ah, I understood your interests lay with Java?" He gave Crane an interrogative and amused look.

"I may not have been strictly accurate with you the last time we met," Crane said. "We need to pick your brains, Town. Can we go in?"

Town's eyebrows rose, if possible, even higher, as he ushered them into his rooms. "My dear fellow. Do I scent a story?"

"A devil of a one. All yours, later. For now, I need some answers. Do you recall when Xan Ji-yin disappeared?"

"Hard to forget," Town said. "The fuss went on for months. We had three or four rounds of guards and shamans asking questions. Didn't you?"

"I wasn't there. I was in the north for a year or more, missed the whole thing."

"Of course. Yes, I recall. Well, I hope you won't ask me to tell you what happened to him, because that's beyond even my knowledge."

"What do you think happened to him?" Stephen asked.

Town gave him a shrewd look. "I couldn't speculate. There were some said he was translated, transfigured, lifted up bodily by the Jade Emperor in the sky, you know. Others thought he'd fallen foul of the emperor on the ground. I never heard a convincing tale. Did you?"

Crane shook his head. "But in any case, I'm not asking you to solve that mystery. This is something else, but around the same time. Did you happen to know any of the people from the Baptist mission?"

Town put a finger on his plump lips. "Mission. The big one on the hill? Yes…"

"There was a girl, or a woman, called Arabella," Crane said. "She also went missing, just before Xan did. I'm hoping to find out her name."

Town took a few thoughtful steps towards the window. "Arabella. Arabella… One wasn't on first-name terms with the ladies, naturally."

"Indeed not," Crane said. "But I can't imagine more than one of them vanished just before Xan did."

"No, of course." Town turned back to face them. "May I ask why?"

"Later. It's a little urgent."

Town's brows went up again. "A girl who's been missing thirteen years is urgent?"

"It's complicated," Crane assured him. "I need to know who she was."

"Was? Is she dead?"

Crane hesitated, shrugged. "So I'm told. Did you know her?"

"Vaguely." Town's normally cheerful face was heavy. "Heavens, Vaudrey, I didn't expect you to bring this up. It was a terrible thing." He took a turn up and down the room, then stopped and put his hand on the back of a chair as if for support. "She went missing, as you say. A very lovely girl, very religious of course, but with so much life. She was in the mission to bring hope and joy, not like most of the crows and vultures that perched there. She was bright, like sunshine. And then she disappeared, and there was a fuss for a few days, and then Xan disappeared and nobody cared about her any more. The officers, the agents, the people—all the resources went to find Xan. She was forgotten. The mission kept looking, for a while, but there were spiteful rumours, slander really, accusations of a man—the usual rubbish—and it was easier for everyone to believe them and forget about her. And then life went on and nobody remembered. You must be the first person in years to have mentioned her."

"What was her name?" Stephen asked.

"Peyton. Arabella Peyton."

"Peyton. *Our* Peyton? That's his—?"

"Sister," Town said. "Or perhaps not, maybe she was too young. His cousin, his niece, I don't know. She was his only family, that I can tell you. He had nobody else. Just the two of them. She came out to

Shanghai to be with him as well as serve her God. And when she vanished, well, it ate away at him, especially with all the people saying she'd run away with a man. He never believed that. He had to stop looking eventually, he kept up the social façade, as it were, but he never forgot her. And I don't suppose he would forgive her killer. No. Never forgive."

Crane nodded. "Thank you, Town. Can I charge you, strongly, to keep this conversation to yourself? I will give you the full story in time, but for now this is not a topic to raise, and particularly not with Peyton. Will he be at the Traders, do you think?"

"He lodges in Hammersmith. King Street, I believe. You should look there first. He's never at the club for luncheon. I hope you don't plan to revive painful memories, Vaudrey, I think he's suffered enough."

"I plan nothing," Crane said. "I just want a word with him. See you later."

"Farewell, dear chap. Nice to see you again, Mr. Day."

CHAPTER FOURTEEN

They walked together out of the house into the baking sunshine as the clocks struck noon.

"Hammersmith, then?" Stephen said.

"Let's drop in at the Traders first. It's on the way, and we can get his direction without having to guess the house number. Well. Peyton. The little shit."

"It sounds like he has reason. Mr. Cryer clearly liked Miss Peyton very much. Did you know her?"

"I didn't mix with the mission people, for obvious reasons. Can you do the silent thing as we walk? So we can talk?"

Stephen hesitated, then gave a twitch of his fingers and the noise of the road dropped away sharply. He was still wearing the Magpie Lord's ring, Crane noted, and felt a pulse of hope.

He took a deep breath. "Listen. I feel—it's a day for painful truths—I need to say something."

"What?" Stephen's voice was wary.

Crane's throat felt uncomfortably dry, and for once, the words didn't come. He had no idea, now, precisely what to say or how, no rehearsed phrases; he simply knew what had to be said.

The hell with it, Vaudrey. Talk.

"Look. I am quite sure I've told you how remarkable you are. I know I have. Magical, and infinitely fuckable, and extraordinarily brave. I'm also well aware that you're a better man than I will ever be. I'm fairly sure you have no idea just how glorious you are, which is fortunate for me, because the more time I have with you, the more aware I am of my own very obvious flaws. And I realise you don't entirely trust me—no, let me say this," he insisted as Stephen tried to interrupt. "I realise that and I don't blame you, but I want—I would like—you to give me a chance to demonstrate that you can. I'm not going back to Shanghai while you will have me here. In fact, I'm not leaving this damned country at all unless you're on the boat with me. I seem to be peculiarly inept at understanding your needs when we're not in bed, and I know I've got a hell of a lot wrong to date, but…don't run away from me, please. Don't disappear."

He looked up at the clear, cloudless sky to avoid Stephen's face. "I recall when Tom first met Leo. Not *first*, but she had gone almost overnight from a gawky schoolgirl to a beauty, and we went to a party at her father's compound. She was quite wonderful, and afterwards Tom was silent for what felt like hours, and then he said to me, 'My life changed tonight.' Well, he had more sense than me, or saw things more clearly. My life changed four months ago, and I utterly failed to understand that until just recently, and therefore…I may have omitted to tell you that I love you." He took a breath. "That's all."

They walked through the crowded streets, side by side, Crane limiting his stride to Stephen's, in silence for a few seconds. When Stephen spoke, his voice was strangled. "Is there a reason you did that in public, when I can't even touch you, let alone—let alone say anything properly?"

"Well, yes. I already know what your cock thinks. I'd like to hear from your head as well. Or your heart."

Stephen kept walking, head down, hands in pockets. Crane could feel his tension, pacing by his side. "Oh God," he said at last. "I'm pathetic. You know perfectly well that I'm all yours, Lucien, or you should. I've got your tattoo, for heaven's sake. I'm marked for life. And I'm scared by that, I'm terrified. I have no idea why you think I'm brave, I'm an abject coward. I'm too frightened to believe this, you and I, can last because if it doesn't, I don't think I can bear it, so it would be easier not to start, but it's too late now." He swallowed. "And it's not that I don't trust you. I just…struggle to believe that someone like you could really want someone like me. No, it's my turn, let me finish. You're an extremely attractive and eligible man, and I'm not. And I seem to do nothing but take from you—"

"No, I can't let that pass, that is objectively horseshit. For heaven's sake, man, I can barely give you the time of day without a fight. Merrick says you're held together by spit and pride."

"Thank him for me." Stephen pushed a hand through his hair. "In any case, that's not the point. I'm not sure what the point was. Oh, hellfire. I love you, Lucien. It wouldn't be so nerve-wracking if I didn't."

Crane took two more paces, feeling the illuminating joy spread through him, and had to control his voice as he observed, "No, you're right, it was a terrible idea to do this in public. I don't suppose you could make us invisible?"

"You must be joking," Stephen said. "Look up."

Crane looked, and groaned aloud as he registered the magpies. They were clustered on gas lamps and roof edges and railings, circling in the skies looking for roosts, a few of them landing in front of him on the pavement, staring with bright, beady eyes. "Oh for— Can't you make them go away?"

"Don't blame me, I didn't call them." Stephen was grinning up at him with that familiar snag-toothed tweak in his top lip, and a light in his golden eyes that made Crane's heart lurch. "And I suspect that anything I attempt to do will light up the street like a bonfire and summon practitioners from miles around. I'm feeling somewhat explosive right now."

"You and me both. I would very much like to get my hands on you."

"I want to get my mouth on you," said Stephen, astonishingly forward considering they weren't in bed, and now it wasn't only Crane's heart that was thumping. "When this is over, could we go away? Your shooting place again?"

"As soon as you like. How long can you take?"

"How long do you want?"

"The rest of your life." Crane watched Stephen's eyes widen. "For now, how about a fortnight?"

"Done," Stephen said. "And…done."

"God, sweet boy. I love you. I think I need to say that quite a lot."

"Any time." Stephen's voice was a little shaky, his eyes bright.

There was a flurry of wings as a group of magpies caught up with them, five landing in a row on the railings, four right in front of them on the pavement. Crane counted automatically and couldn't help grinning. "Look at that. Do the damned things know the rhymes?"

"I hope not. It's nine for a funeral, isn't it?"

Crane let the back of his hand brush Stephen's arm. "Try, 'Nine for a lover as true as can be'."

"Oh. I like your version better." Stephen bumped gently back against him, a little touch, nothing to which an observer could object. "Here's the Traders."

Crane slowed his pace as they approached the square brick building. "I want this business over. I think I could feel sorry for Peyton, you know, and that's not something I'd often say."

"So could I. But I bet Mr. Trotter couldn't. Lucien, I want you to come to Hammersmith with me. You don't have to talk to Peyton, or even witness the conversation, since I doubt it'll be pretty, but I want you to stay close. And you can wipe that smirk off. I *meant*, in case of rats."

"Rats? Me?"

Stephen shrugged. "You were Hart's friend. I don't know how far this will go. Humour me."

Crane lifted an acknowledging hand. "If you insist on me not dying horribly, I suppose I'll have to indulge you." He led the way into the relative cool of the entrance hall and nodded to the porter. "Hello, Arthurs. Can you whistle up Mr. Peyton's direction for me?"

"Certainly, my lord, but do you want to speak to him? He's lunching upstairs."

Crane glanced at Stephen. "Really? That's a stroke of luck. Yes, we'll go up, never mind the direction."

"What would you like to do now?" Stephen asked quietly. "Stay down here if it's too close to home."

"No, I'll come with you. It might be easier to get a word in private that way."

They headed up the stairs together, Crane torn between a flinching distaste for the job ahead and the temptation to head for the bar and order champagne. It had doubtless been a crashingly inappropriate time to raise the subject of their relationship, but now… He didn't have to watch that look of pain and loneliness come back to Stephen's eyes. He could take away the money worries, the fear of arrest, the quiet, constant fretting about a lonely future. He could treat Stephen as he deserved, and what was for certain, he would find a way to make sure the little sod was curled up in his bed every night, returning home to him, instead of vanishing wordlessly off to unexplained dangers. *My little witch. Mine.* He suppressed the urge to whistle

"You look like the cat that swallowed the cream," Stephen said softly.

"That comes later. Here's the dining room."

The small-windowed room with its dark wood furnishings looked particularly dingy against the bright sunshine outside. Peyton was sitting alone with a newspaper. He didn't look happy to see Crane as they walked up to his table.

"Vaudrey. Oh, I beg your pardon, *Lord* Crane." He gave the usual sneer. "And your little friend."

"Can we have a word with you?"

Peyton shrugged. "If you must. What is it?"

"In private, please," Stephen said.

"I don't particularly want to speak to you in private." Peyton rustled his paper pointedly. "I'm waiting for my luncheon."

Stephen put a hand on Peyton's. "Listen to me. Get up and come with us now."

Peyton got up immediately and followed as Crane led them to one of the small studies. Stephen came last, shutting the door, as Peyton blinked in surprise to find himself there.

"Mr. Peyton. Tell me about Arabella."

Peyton stared. "Who?"

"Your relative Arabella."

"What about her?"

"When did you find out she was dead?"

Peyton's brow furrowed. "Well, when my sister wrote to me, of course."

"Your sister," repeated Stephen.

"Yes. Maria. Great-Aunt Belle lived with her, till she dropped off her perch. What the devil does my family have to do with you?"

"Family?" said Crane.

Stephen held Peyton's gaze. "I want to know about your female relative from the Baptist mission in Shanghai."

"We're Anglicans," Peyton said. "I don't have any relatives in Shanghai. Never did. And—"

"Have you many here?"

"Four sisters and their children. Look here, I don't—"

"Shit," said Crane. "*Shit*. Stephen…"

"I know. Mr. Peyton, were you in Shanghai when Xan Ji-yin disappeared?"

"What?"

"*Answer me!*" Stephen shouted, making both the other men jump.

"Yes, I—" Peyton began in wounded tones.

"Do you remember a girl who went missing from the Baptist mission?"

"Is that what this is about? Town's sister? Lord, yes, she ran off with some man, didn't she? At least, *I* heard—"

Stephen turned and bolted for the door, Crane at his heels. They took the stairs two at a time, and Crane nearly tripped over Stephen as he stopped at the bottom. "Send a note to Esther at the surgery," he said shortly. "Tell them all to meet us at Cryer's lodgings. Catch me up."

"Take a cab." Crane fumbled for a handful of change. "I'm sorry, Stephen."

"My responsibility." Stephen grabbed the money and darted outside.

Crane scrawled the note and paid a messenger lavishly to get it there as fast as possible, then hailed a hackney himself, cursing foully. It hadn't occurred to him to doubt Town: the man had always been part of the scenery, a reliable gossip, something of a joke. He observed and relayed events; he didn't take part in them.

But he had sent them off on a wild-goose chase after a man he knew Crane disliked. And Crane should have known there was something wrong with his tale of the solitary man and his only relative because he'd bloody met Peyton's bloody nephew—at this point he banged his head, hard, against the side of the carriage—and now he had comprehensively let Stephen down. Fuck.

He believed part of Town's story though. The beloved sister, the lifetime of bitterness. That had rung very true. He could imagine how it would feel to have someone you love vanish forever—he had imagined it, he realised, that time Stephen had gone off after a warlock and not come back for four days without a word. And to have men like

Peyton cast casual aspersions on a loved sister's honour must have been gall in the wound, even before Town knew she was dead.

Who had told him?

The cab stopped, and Crane hurried up the steps to Town's lodgings. The housekeeper let him in without argument, a blank look in her eyes. Stephen was using fluence with abandon, it seemed.

Town's door was open.

"Don't come in," called Stephen from within as Crane strode up. "He's long gone. I'm trying to ascertain where. Not very good at it, I need Esther's nose. Can you stay outside? You play hob with everything."

That, discretion aside, meant that Stephen was interrogating the ether for traces of Town. He had occasionally mentioned that Crane's etheric presence was extremely strong, pulling the imperceptible currents towards him. Yu Len, a Chinese shaman, had always said Crane had powerful *ch'i*, but it had never actually caused a problem before.

Feeling that he'd done enough damage for one day, Crane retreated obediently outside and stood, waiting, estimating how long it would take the other justiciars to arrive, wondering what they would do with Leonora. What he really wanted to think about was whether Stephen would agree to move his home to Crane's rooms in the Strand, but under the circumstances that felt like tempting fate.

He was staring out into the road when a cab pulled up further down and Monk Humphris got out.

Monk seemed fretful and worried, as he had for weeks. He marched up towards Town's lodgings, brows close. Crane lifted a hand in greeting, and, since that failed to catch the man's eye, called, "Hoi, Monk!"

Monk looked up and saw him. His whole face changed to a mask of horror as he registered Crane outside Town's building. Then he turned and fled down the street.

Crane was after him before he had time to think. It wasn't a rational decision. Monk ran and Crane chased, his mind catching up with his body as he ran.

This was probably stupid. Probably pointless. But Stephen could follow him if he had to, and better he should get hold of Monk and find him irrelevant than let another lead go.

And it wasn't pointless. Why would Monk run if he didn't have to? The heat thundered on the back of Crane's neck and beat down on his light grey suit, rapidly getting sweat-soaked. Merrick would murder him. Stephen had told him, long ago, "no Savile Row" when they faced running for their lives; as his expensive shoes slithered on the paving stones, he recalled the truth of that.

Monk was tiring now, shoulders heaving, steps slowing. He cornered desperately into an alley. Crane put on a burst of speed, long legs giving him an advantage as ever, swung round the corner, hurdled a pile of rubbish that Monk had knocked across the way, and grabbed the man by his shoulder.

Monk, gasping, turned. He was trying to fight but he looked exhausted.

"Pack it in," Crane panted. "What the hell, Monk?"

"Go away," Monk managed, between heaving breaths. "In God's name, go, man. Run. *Run!*"

"Why?"

Monk stared at him, wide eyed. He took a single sucking breath. Then his pupils contracted, vanishing to pinpoints, so that his eyes were blank and staring. Something dreadful, fear and pain, swept across his face and vanished, leaving only a featureless acceptance. He focused his unseeing gaze on Crane, and hissed, "*Shaman.*"

"What?" said Crane. "I'm not."

"Shaman," repeated Monk, sniffing, his nose wriggling with hideous mobility, greed blossoming in his dead eyes.

"No." Crane took a step back, wanting to run, suddenly realising what a bad mistake this had been. "Monk?"

"Power." Monk spoke in Shanghainese. "Strength and joy and *ch'i*. So much. Yes, this will do."

He reached out a clawed hand. Crane took another step back, then finally obeyed his screaming instincts, turned, and bolted, right into Town Cryer, who grabbed him by the arm.

"You stupid bloody fool," said Town, and everything went black.

CHAPTER FIFTEEN

Crane blinked back to consciousness because of the pain, and wished he hadn't.

His arms hurt like hell, his shoulders shrieking. This was, he realised, because his wrists were tied to the wall behind him, arms high and wide, crucifixion-style. His unsupported body had lolled forward so that all thirteen stone hung off his shoulder muscles, and his arms were bending backwards.

His ankles were tied, but he got his feet under him, straightened till they took his weight, and felt the agonising fire in his shoulders damp to a mere inferno.

He was in some kind of cavern. A cellar? It was cool, dark, earthy-smelling. A lantern sat on the earth floor and illuminated whitewashed but rough and grubby walls. There was a sturdy table placed in front of him, and on the far side of the room was a door made of dark wood, reinforced with a thick wooden bar that sat across the frame.

Monk was walking around the cellar, muttering, but it wasn't Monk. Crane didn't need a practitioner to tell him that. The jerky movement, the hideous facial twitching, the light in the blank eyes, none of those belonged to the body being jerked around like an ungainly puppet.

Is there someone in there?

Town was squatting against the wall, Chinese style, face in hands.

"Oi," Crane said. "What the devil is this?"

Town looked up. "Vaudrey. You had to interfere, didn't you? You couldn't just go away. I told you to go to Hammersmith, damn it! Why didn't you go to Hammersmith?"

"Shitty luck." Crane's voice was hoarse and dry. "You tried to kill Leo Hart. With rats."

"She deserves it."

"The hell she does. Rackham, those two so-called shamans, yes, but not Leo, and not a houseful of people on Ratcliffe Highway."

"Who cares about them?" Town snapped, but his eyes flicked away as he spoke.

"Stephen Day does. Remember him? Short chap, reddish hair, one of the most dangerous men in London, on his way here right now to rip your spine out through your arsehole. So, who's in Monk?" Crane looked over at the man's awful, mad twitching. "Xan Ji-yin, I presume?"

Monk threw back his head and howled. His jaw seemed to unhinge, stretching wide and gaping, like a snake.

"Nice." Crane had to keep talking, because otherwise he was liable to piss himself with terror. "Charming friends you have, Town."

"This is what happens when you treat people like offal." Town spoke with concentrated vitriol. "That bastard Hart and his madmen murdered my sister and Xan Ji-yin and threw them into the water like dead dogs. If they'd had decent burial— Well, those swine are paying now."

"Rackham and the shamans have certainly paid," Crane said. "More power to your elbow. Why am *I* here?"

"He wants you." Town jerked his head towards Monk.

"Him? That? Why?"

"He needs a suitable body." Town licked his lips. His face was under control but his eyes were full of horror. "And normal people won't do. They die, you see, all of them. He's been through body after body, but with the best will in the world, they just don't do, not once he starts using them, and he can't live in corpses. He was in Monk for a while without him noticing, but now… Poor Monk. But he knew Bella, he liked her. He wouldn't have minded, really."

"Really?" said Crane, watching Monk's neck muscles distort as the thing inside his body raged.

"And now he wants you. Apparently you're a shaman. That's what he needs. I didn't know you were a shaman."

"I'm bloody not!"

"He says you are. He wants you. When he's finished here and he's got a shaman host, he'll go away, and it will all be over, at last. I'm sorry, Vaudrey, but you should have gone to Hammersmith. I did try and tell you. And you were thick as thieves with Hart—"

"I was a thousand miles away when your sister died," Crane said. "The first I heard of it was this morning. Town, for God's sake, don't let it do this!"

Town was shaking his head. "It's too late. Xan Ji-yin needs a body with shaman powers, and you have them, that's all." He shrugged one shoulder with a tip of the head, a characteristic little gesture Crane had seen his friend make hundreds of times. "I'm sorry, my dear fellow. If you don't fight, I think it will be quick."

"That fucking thing is not taking my fucking body." Crane's mouth could barely work with the terror. He had seen shamanic possession reduce Merrick to a drooling imbecile, had had his mind repeatedly attacked, had even had his memories violated by Stephen once. The thought of the foul thing inside Monk moving to his own mind dizzied him with horror and fear. "You're making a bad mistake. Stephen's a shaman. A real one, not a fucking travesty like that reject from a charnel house. You touch me, he will hunt you to the grave. You won't know what vengeance is till he comes after you."

"I know vengeance," Town said. "Hart's dead. Xan has killed Rackham and Pa and Lo. Now he's going to walk out of here wearing you like a coat, and that's how he'll finish Leonora Hart off, and I hope Hart looks up from hell to see it."

"You bastard." Crane thrashed and strained against the ropes, but it was no good, the bonds were tight and secure. Town got up and spoke to Monk, quietly. Then he picked up a small bowl and a knife and walked over to place them on the table. He undid one of Crane's cuffs and rolled the sleeve back.

He took up the bowl and the knife again. "We'll need some of your blood for this," he explained, and sliced into Crane's forearm.

Crane yelled, with the pain, and in the hope of attracting attention. The blood ran down his arm, splashing into the bowl Town held, unnaturally fast, too much of it, pouring out from the minor wound as though an artery had been cut. "Blood magic?" he snarled. "You're a fucking warlock without even being a shaman. Stephen is going to kill you, and then bring you back from the dead just to kill you again, you son of a bitch!"

"I suppose he's your new bed boy." Town placed the full bowl carefully on the table. "They don't usually stay around when things get difficult, do they?" He took a roll of bandage and started to wind it around the wound.

Crane spat in his face. Town's mouth tightened as he wiped the spittle away. "Don't do that," he said. "This isn't my fault."

The thing in Monk's body came up to the table, facing Crane, as Town finished with the bandage. Its face was moving and jerking continually, lines and creases running across it, lips twitching and mumbling.

Crane pulled violently against the ropes that bound him, knowing it was no use.

Monk raised his hands in a gesture that looked entirely Chinese, entirely shamanical, and the blood in the bowl began to stir, first rippling, then bubbling. The red darkened, cloudy brown swirls appearing through it.

Crane was thrashing now, desperate, helpless, crying out with fury. It was so damned, bloody unfair, that he should die now, or worse than die, should lose his mind to this creature, without having kissed Stephen again or even held him. It was no consolation at all that he'd told the man he loved him or heard it in return. All it meant was a full, agonising knowledge of what he was going to lose.

Nine for a funeral.

The infected blood in the bowl was rising up now in a shape like a waterspout, a rotten dark brown, defying all nature, and as Crane stared at it, he felt the ghost's invasion.

It was filthy. A choking charnel foulness like thick wet cobweb, over his face and eyes and mouth, crawling in his ears, up his nose, through his body. He tried to scream and the tendrils dug deeper. He could hear an insane muttering in his mind, fragments of rage and fury and accusation and a horrible glee as the thing tapped into somewhere deep and wrenched. The power lit in his blood, but it was snatched greedily, dragging at his flesh and bones, nothing like what Stephen did. This was a rape. He shook his head violently because he could do nothing else, and the dead man's soul settled to feed, pushing a film over his eyes as he stared in helpless horror at the bowl of foaming, churning blood.

The spout jerked abruptly. It straightened again, steadied, then lurched sideways once more, and streaks of red shone bright through the dirty brown. Monk, standing like a puppet with loose strings, jerked too, lifting his head. The spout began to spasm, more violently, whipping from side to side, its rhythm breaking and restabilising and breaking again. Xan's ghost gave a terrible keening howl and dug impalpable claws into Crane's mind, but he could feel the other pull now. It was rushing through his veins in a storm of black and white wings, and from somewhere deep inside, he welcomed it, reached out, let the birds take over.

I am the Magpie Lord, he insisted to himself, through Xan's screams. We *are the Magpie Lord. Let them fly, Stephen, fly with them, and get this monster out of my mind!*

Xan's talons dug into him with a desperate effort. Crane yelled aloud, a cry of pain and defiance that was echoed by the shrieks of birds that weren't there, the sharp stabbing of beaks, the thunder of invisible wings beating around and through him.

The bowl exploded. Shards of earthenware went flying across the room, and the blood sprayed into a bright red cloud, in which hung, for just a fraction of a second, the image of a bird, before the spray dissipated into nothing. The creature in Crane's body was ripped away, howling. Crane gasped for breath, head stabbing with sudden agony. Monk began to scream in earnest. And the thick wooden door burst inwards as though punched by a giant's fist.

Stephen came in running, ducking through the splinters, Esther Gold just behind him. He threw out a hand as he ran, sending Monk tumbling backwards, and sprinted towards Crane, eyes blazing gold and black in his white face. Town cried out in rage and pulled a pistol, and an urchin boy—no, it was Jenny Saint in trousers and a cap—ran at him, up through the air, as if mounting invisible steps, and kicked him ferociously in the face. Town fell, and she landed on him hard and booted his hand, sending the gun skittering across the floor.

Janossi, Merrick and Leonora were in now. Merrick saw his master, swore with gusto and ran forward. Leonora followed, pausing to kick Town in the balls with force and accuracy. Stephen turned away from Monk, looking up at Crane, starting to speak, but Crane only had eyes for Monk's slumped body. His old friend looked like himself once more with no alien consciousness there, and Crane gathered every scrap of strength he had left to bellow, "*Rats!*"

There was a fractional moment of total stillness. Then the rats came.

They flooded in from every corner and crevice. Not the few that had almost killed Leo, but hundreds, tumbling over one another, growing as he watched, flinging themselves forward with snarls like dogs. They met a wave of power from Esther and Stephen which flung them over and over backwards, and bounced up and came on again, with a dreadful shrill squealing and a scrape and dry rustle of claws on earth and stone.

"Get him free!" Stephen yelled at Merrick, as Esther shoved Leonora behind her. The four justiciars formed a semicircle in front of Crane, shoulder to shoulder, hurling power. A rat leapt at Esther and its skull exploded like a rotten orange. Behind them, Merrick hopped up onto the table with his pocketknife in his hand, and began to saw at the thick ropes that pinioned Crane.

"Hoi!" he shouted at Leonora. "Up here, give me a hand." He pulled out another knife. "And you, Vaudrey, on your feet."

"You try," slurred Crane, stiffening his legs under him as best he could to stop his body slumping.

"Shit." Merrick was working furiously. "The fuck did they do to you?"

"Put that thing in me. Shaman ghost."

"Fuck."

"S'alright."

"It's not," said Leonora grimly, sawing at his other wrist.

Crane looked round her. The rats were filling the room now, in their hundreds, clambering over each other with savage, single-minded killing determination. The four justiciars were holding their ground, somehow keeping a corridor of space in front of themselves, but there were so many rats that the pile of dead was two feet deep already and the creatures kept on coming. A rat leapt over the top, over their heads, its limbs spread wide in attack. Saint rose high in the air to punch it away, and the other three all cried, "Hold the line!", swaying back in unison.

Crane glanced to his left and yelled, "Janossi!"

The man had good reflexes, which saved his life. He didn't look at Crane but to his other side, and that meant he was able to twist away from Town's attack so that the blade aimed at his heart scraped off ribs and stabbed the flesh below his shoulder.

Janossi bellowed with pain and released a bolt of power that sent Town flying back into the wall, and as he did so, the rats surged in.

"Hold the damned line!" Stephen screamed. "Resonance three over eight and *go*."

All four justiciars hissed indrawn breaths in violent unison. A terrible high-pitched vibration filled Crane's head. Leonora clapped her free hand to one ear, twisting her neck in a fruitless effort to turn away from the sound. The pitch rose slightly higher and became a feeling, a buzzing in the teeth and eyeballs. The rats hauled back, hesitating, squealing in confusion, and Saint gave a savage cry of triumph as the justiciars pushed forward at a command from Esther, sending rat parts flying, but the creatures turned again in a smoothly coordinated wave and reattacked with as much savagery as before.

"Will you cut that blasted rope!" Stephen shouted.

"Nearly there, sir," called Merrick, sawing patiently away with the knife.

Knife.

Town had held the knife competently, a man who knew how to stab someone to death…

"Why did they kill Willetts?" Crane asked aloud.

"Who gives a fuck?" grunted Merrick. "*Yes.*" The thick rope parted, the last strands breaking as he and Crane wrenched at it. Merrick immediately moved to help Leonora with the other rope.

"He doesn't need a spell, look at him." *He* was Xan; Crane was not going to speak that name aloud. "And he doesn't need an amulet to control the rats, either. So why kill Willetts? What did Willetts know?"

"The story?"

"The ending," Crane said, with sudden certainty. "The real ending. The girl, the vessel of the Red Tide. Of course."

He glanced at Stephen, but the justiciars were fighting for their lives now, no time to talk. Janossi fell to one knee and Esther hauled him up, but it cost her a step back.

"Fuck." Crane wrenched at his pinioned hand but it wasn't even close to free, so he made a decision, gave the order.

"Merrick. Kill Mr. Humphris. Strangle him. No blood."

Merrick stopped sawing at the rope. He met Crane's eyes, his face emotionless.

"*Now*," Crane said.

Merrick folded his pocketknife and put it in Crane's free hand. "Anyone got a bit of string?"

"There's a handkerchief in my pocket."

"Here." Leonora kicked off her shoe and dragged off a torn silk stocking. "I hope you know what you're doing."

Merrick took the stocking and jumped down from the table, pulling a pencil from one of his pockets. He went to Monk where he lay by the wall and pulled the recumbent man to a kneeling posture. He slipped the stocking round his neck with the pencil inside the loop, and began to tighten the makeshift garrotte, face remote and calm.

"Oh God, Lucien," Leonora whispered.

"Keep cutting." Crane's own hand was shaking so hard he'd be in danger of slicing an artery if he tried to help.

Monk seemed unconscious, but as Merrick tightened the rope he began to jerk and struggle, as if by instinct. Every rat in the room froze, suddenly stiff. And then, as one, they all poured towards Merrick.

"Sodding hell!" said Saint, who was at that side of the room. She staggered backwards under the huge weight of rodent fury, the invisible shields bowing under the pressure. Esther and Stephen both hurled themselves sideways towards her, Janossi a fraction later, and now all four justiciars were jumbled in front of Merrick, and the corridor of protective space between them and the rats was down to inches and bending backwards as the rats piled three, four feet high. Claws and teeth scrabbled savagely as the rats screamed their rage. Monk kicked and spasmed, eyes bulging, face blackening, and the justiciars were all shouting, and Crane's other hand came free. He fell forward, chest hitting the table in front of him, and lay over it gasping for breath.

Monk's tongue protruded, face suffused, eyes popping, and from the jerking of his body, Crane knew his feet were drumming on the floor. Quite suddenly, he went limp.

The rats all screamed at once. It rang through Crane's bones and his eyes and his hair, a wrenching agony, and then, abruptly, it stopped, and the rats were tumbling away, retreating, shrinking.

"Jesus." Crane slid off the table and onto the floor. He saw the live rats fleeing through holes in the walls, the dead ones deflating like pricked bladders.

"Lucien!" There was a scrape as Stephen shoved the table out of the way. He looked grey with exhaustion. "Lucien, are you all right?"

"Fine. Well, not fine. Alive."

Stephen dropped to his knees in front of him and took his chin in a gentle hand. Crane leaned slightly forward to turn the touch to a hold, aware of the others, but needing the comfort, and felt Stephen cup his face tenderly even as he turned it from side to side, examining Crane's eyes.

"I thought we agreed you weren't going to be horribly killed. I'm sure you said that."

"I said I wasn't going to be horribly killed *by rats*. I never promised not to have my soul eaten by a demented ghost." Crane was trying for humour but his voice cracked betrayingly. "God. I've never wanted to see anyone so much in my life."

"I'm glad we were here in time." Stephen spoke mildly, but his grip belied the calm of his words.

Crane looked around. Merrick was watching, unharmed. He gave Crane a nod as their eyes met. The dead rats were in piles, shrinking, not as fast as the live ones had. He abruptly became aware of the choking stench of their foul bodies, sewer filth and rodent piss. Janossi was slumped on the floor with Leo holding a handkerchief to his wound; Saint was vomiting noisily in a corner. Esther sat back on her heels, looking lined and drained.

"Is it over?" said Crane.

"It is for them," Esther said. "Tell me, Mr. Merrick, why did you kill him?" She jerked her head over in Monk's direction.

"Is that a problem, madam?" enquired Merrick without inflection.

"No, it's a question. How did you know what to do?"

"I told him to do it," Crane said. "My responsibility." His ankles were still pinioned, he realised. He sat back, shifted his legs forward and started to saw at the rope with the pocketknife. Stephen silently took it from his hand and bent to the work.

"And?"

Crane cautiously flexed a shoulder. His throat was horribly dry. "Willetts. You speculated he was killed by someone needing the chant or the amulet. But clearly the shaman, that thing, *didn't* need them. So why kill him? I concluded he was stabbed to shut him up. Not about the story, everyone already knew that, but for the thing he knew and nobody else did. The real ending."

His voice cracked. Merrick threw him a hip flask, and he took a gulp of raw brandy. "Christ! Steal the good stuff next time, you know where it is." He handed it on to Stephen. "When we first heard the story, it all ended when the vessel of the Red Tide was strangled. No blood. I thought perhaps that was what they wanted to hide. The ghost needed blood to move into me. And if its host body was killed without bloodshed—well, Town said Xan couldn't live in a corpse."

"I see." Esther took the flask from Stephen and swigged. "That's a devil of a deductive leap. How were you sure your version of the ending was the true one?"

"I wasn't. That was a calculated risk."

She threw back her head with a sudden crack of laughter. "Magnificent. It's a pleasure doing business with you, Lord Crane."

Crane forced himself to control his voice. "The man I just had killed was named Paul Humphris. Monk, we called him. He had no part in this. Town trapped him for that damned creature's use. He tried to warn me to run, before that thing took him over. He was a *friend*."

Stephen paused in his work to put a hand on his arm, warning. Esther said, "I'm sorry. But you should know, you didn't kill him. The possession destroyed his mind, and his body wouldn't have survived long after it. Your friend was already gone."

"I saw him earlier today," Crane said obstinately. "He was himself. He spoke to me."

Stephen gave his arm a gentle stroke. "Things like that can squat in the mind, almost unnoticed, almost harmless, for a very long time. Like a toad, or a cancer. I'd imagine that it simply roosted in Mr. Humphris when it wasn't controlling the rats. It's only when they take over the body that they destroy the original inhabitant, root out the brain and the soul and the nerves and replace them. There's no coming back from that."

Crane recalled Monk's body, the ugly jerking. "It was moving him like a puppet. A meat puppet. It was going to do that to me, wasn't it?"

"Not on my time." Stephen cut through the last few strands of the rope, dropped the knife, and brushed his hands over Crane's abused ankles with a gesture that looked professional and felt anything but. "You are, I think, fine. No damage done. Mr. Merrick, were you hurt?"

"No, sir."

"Joss?"

"Flesh wound."

"Bleeding wound," Stephen said. "You'd have been next up for possession, because you let yourself get stabbed. You have to pay more attention."

"Sir."

"And while I'm on the subject of attention, when I say three over eight I *mean* three over eight, and not somewhere between three and a half and four," Stephen added. "I've never heard such a racket. Do we need to go over resonance again, Saint?"

"We was a bit busy," Saint muttered.

"You'll always be busy. And then you'll be dead because you can't get a simple resonance right. Both of you go to Mr. Maupert tomorrow, and don't come back till you can give me three over eight for five minutes, understood?"

"Sir," mumbled the two juniors in chorus. Saint went on, "But Mrs. Gold doesn't—"

"When you can do what Mrs. Gold does, you can decide for yourself what's important," Stephen said. "In the meantime, resonance."

"Enliven your lessons by meditating on the words *hold the line*," Esther added. "That was shambolic, Saint. Otherwise, though, not bad work, you two. We would still have had our backsides kicked without Lord Crane, of course."

"The reverse is significantly more the case," Crane said. "I'm indebted to you all."

"So am I," said Leonora quietly. "This was my fault, Tom's fault. I'm sorry."

That was greeted with silence, because there wasn't much to say to it. Crane looked round. "Town?"

"Dead," Esther said.

"What? How?"

"Poison. He seems to have taken something very unpleasant and very fast acting. No blood. I don't think he wanted to be Xan's next host."

"Jesus. What are we going to do about him?" Crane asked. "About all this mess?"

Stephen opened his mouth, but Esther interrupted him firmly. "That's my decision. Mr. Merrick, I need an able-bodied man. Can I call on you?"

"By all means, madam."

"Good. Joss, take Mrs. Hart to the surgery. You can wash there and borrow another dress," she told Leonora. "While she changes, Joss, get yourself stitched up, then escort her home. But send for Inspector Rickaby first and have him directed here. Got it? Good. Steph, I want to be sure Lord Crane's free of that thing. Get him home and keep an eye on him overnight, please. Saint, you, me and Mr. Merrick will tidy up here."

"How's that fair?" grumbled Saint.

"At what point did I promise you fair? You have your jobs, go."

"Yes, ma'am." Stephen was wearing one of his blander expressions.

Merrick came over and offered Crane a hand, pulling him to his feet. "You all right?"

"Yes. You?"

"Course."

Crane nodded, gripping Merrick's hand for a second's silent connection. The manservant patted him on the arm. "Off you go now, my lord. All done here."

CHAPTER SIXTEEN

They emerged up a flight of stairs, through a clean but bare house, and out into the late afternoon light together. Crane had had no idea where he was or how long he had been in the cellar, but now he looked around with a frown. "Are we in Holborn?"

"Not far off. Can you walk home? It would be better if you could, to get your body feeling more normal. Exercise will be good for it," Stephen added demurely. "Joss, take Mrs. Hart in a cab. At least— Lord Crane…"

Crane found a couple of shillings in his pocket. "Here you go. Be good, Leo. I'll see you tomorrow."

"Are you all right, Lucien?" she demanded. "You look dreadful."

"Thank you, *adai*. I'll be fine once I get into bed."

"I'm sure you will." She flashed him a little smile. "Tomorrow, then."

"You don't feel she might need someone with her?" asked Stephen as they walked away. "She must be feeling terribly guilty."

"She'll live. Leo never had any more morals than Tom, not really."

"Hart had a lot to answer for," said Stephen grimly. "That poor lost soul."

"Monk?"

"Xan."

"What?"

"Do you believe in hell?" Stephen said abruptly.

"No, not really. Should I?"

Stephen shrugged. "I don't believe in demons and pitchforks. But I think, if you had to define hell, you could take a good man and deny him the rites he believed in, and condemn his soul to a slow process of madness and vengeance and corruption until it was nothing but a mass of rage and hate and seething evil that his true self would have loathed. I think that would be hell." He took a few more steps, accompanied by Crane's appalled silence. "I don't know, of course. Never met the man. Maybe he went so bad because he was flawed. Or, maybe what we encountered had no consciousness left from what he used to be. I hope it didn't."

Crane swallowed. "Do you think—there are prayers, rituals. If they were done, even without a body, would that help him now?"

"I've no idea," Stephen said. "It couldn't hurt."

"No. I'll see them done. For Xan Ji-yin, and Arabella Cryer, and poor bloody Monk. And Town, too. Do you think he meant to do it all, or was he made to?"

Stephen sighed. "Everyone can do evil. Some people can be forced to it, and some fight against it, and some don't even need an invitation. I imagine Mr. Cryer made a choice initially; I don't suppose he understood the consequences of that choice any more than Pa and Lo and Rackham did."

They walked on through the hot streets, Crane felt better with each step, as his muscles moved and worked and loosened and the summer sun warmed his skin. He was also ravenously hungry, he realised, and had no doubt that Stephen was the same, but there was no point suggesting they stop to eat. His pockets were bare, and he was well aware of the glances of amazed revulsion they were garnering, as people veered away from the stench, then realised just how well dressed one of the stinking men was.

"Good God, I want to wash."

"Wash. Eat." Stephen glanced up at him. "And so on."

That forced Crane to ask the question. "Stephen. The truth, please. Is that thing—could it be still in me?"

"What? No, of course not. If I thought it was, we wouldn't be strolling home now."

"Yes, but how can you be sure? What if it left something in me, and we fucked and it got at you—"

"First," Stephen said firmly, "if it had got a grip on you, we'd all be dead. That thing, with your potential? It would have been a bloodbath. Second, I know it's not in you because I was in you too. For which thank God, because if I hadn't had your blood in my veins today, I wouldn't have known what it was doing in time, or stood a chance of beating it. But I did, and I won, and it's gone. Trust me."

Crane nodded, assimilating that, feeling the fear fade. "So you fought it, fought over me, in my blood?"

"More or less. Lit the power up, called the magpies."

"I know, I felt it, but…didn't that make you vulnerable to it? If it had won, and you were in my blood—"

"Oh, well, that makes no difference," Stephen said hastily. "If something of that malevolence had got hold of the Magpie Lord's power it would have been a disaster of epic proportions, so preventing that was the important thing."

"I beg to differ. Christ, Stephen. Come home with me, and this time, don't leave."

Crane's mansion flat on the Strand had, among its other luxuries, a tiled bathroom, with water piped in. It was cold, since the boiler wasn't on, but Stephen sat by the basin with a hand dangling in the water, which bubbled gently against his fingers till the steam rose.

Crane watched him. "God, you're useful. Useful, beautiful, remarkable."

"Washable," Stephen said. "I want to throw this suit away, I think."

"I've wanted you to do that for months."

They stripped off their bloody, rat-stinking clothes, and Stephen grabbed the heap and dropped them outside the back kitchen door. Crane took the opportunity to start washing, soaping and sluicing himself, scrubbing his contaminated skin with a rough sponge.

"I'll do your back," said Stephen softly, behind him.

Crane hooked over a stool with his foot and sat. Stephen's hands prickled and feathered over his back, slick with soap, sliding down his flanks, working round to caress his chest. His fingertips closed on Crane's nipples, rolling and working them, and Crane moaned and leaned back against him. Stephen slid down, so his breath was hot on Crane's back and a warm tongue flickered against the top of Crane's arse and down between his buttocks, as Stephen's hands roamed over his thighs, then very deliberately brushed the tip of his straining cock.

Crane groaned. "Dirty little witch."

"All true," Stephen murmured, his fingertips dancing, spangling lightning through Crane's cock. "If you washed me, I wouldn't be dirty."

"You'll always be dirty to me." Crane pulled him round. Stephen fell willingly into his lap, arching his back to offer himself up, and Crane grabbed the soap and began to run it over his chest, dipping and flicking water to work up a lather. He lavished attention on those sensitive hands till Stephen moaned audibly, then worked his way slowly down the little man's narrow torso to the jutting hip bones and dark reddish curls at his crotch.

Crane angled the soap and slid it gently along the crack of Stephen's arse, feeling him writhe at the tease. He dipped a finger in the lather and drew delicate patterns on Stephen's skin, sliding down and around, under and over, watching him twitch and whimper. "God, you're beautiful," he said. "Tell me what you want."

"I want you, my lord," Stephen said hoarsely. "I want you to fuck me and not let go. I love you."

"I love you too." Crane stroked a hand over Stephen's hair and gave him a wry smile. "My hero."

"I was terrified." The words were blurted out. Crane's fingers stilled as Stephen's golden eyes met his, their expression suddenly raw. "I thought I'd lost you, Lucien. I thought I'd find that thing wearing your body and eating your mind, and I couldn't bear it. Oh God."

"Come here." Crane brought Stephen upright on his lap and held him close. Stephen bowed his head. Crane could feel him shaking as the day's tension finally caught up with him, and wrapped both arms round his lover, pressing his mouth to Stephen's hair.

Stephen gave a little gulp. "Sorry. Sorry. I just…"

"Ssh. It's all right, sweetheart. I'm not going anywhere. Take your time."

They were silent for a while, Stephen taking long, shallow breaths as he tried to regain control. Crane held him and listened and finally heard the quick, sharp inhalation that signalled his lover pulling himself together.

"All right?"

"Yes. I'm sorry, that was an ill-timed fit of vapours."

"We've got all night. Have all the vapours you want."

Stephen snuggled closer. Crane stroked his hair, ran his fingers over the tips of his ears and brushed them down over his earlobes. "It's all right," he murmured. "Everything's all right."

"Now it is. It's been such a horrible day," Stephen said plaintively, into his chest.

"Oh, I don't know. It had its moments."

"True. The moments were wonderful. But I'd quite like to forget a lot of the hours."

"That can be arranged. Whenever you're ready." Crane drew a fingernail down the nape of Stephen's neck, watching him shiver.

"Mmm. Thank you, Lucien."

"What for?"

"I don't know. Being here."

"Well, that's your fault," Crane pointed out. "You keep saving my skin."

Stephen looked up, lopsided grin dawning. "But it's such marvellously decorative skin. It would be a pity to waste it."

Crane pulled Stephen into a deep kiss at that, hands roaming, feeling the electric prickle in his response. He stroked and licked and bit, not allowing his lover to start thinking again, gently readying the man till Stephen was squirming on his lap in helpless reaction.

"Lucien, my lord, my lord…"

"Mmm?" murmured Crane invitingly.

"Now. Please. Fuck me. Lots."

"We are going to fuck till you forget your own name, but…" Crane couldn't imagine anything he wanted less than to manhandle Stephen, not today. "I want you in charge." He smiled at Stephen's startled expression. His lover had an uncompromising preference for being on the receiving end, and that suited Crane well, but it was about time Stephen broadened his experience a little. "Come here, witch. Take me inside you."

"*Oh.*" Stephen scrambled into position on his lap, lowered himself carefully towards Crane's straining cock, and clutched his shoulders for balance as he eased himself down. "Mmm."

"However you like," Crane murmured, kissing Stephen's neck and shoulder, keeping his own hips still. "You set the pace. You're in control. Take it exactly as you want."

"I'm starting to wonder if there *is* someone else in there," Stephen muttered, sliding down a careful, agonising inch or so. Crane began to stretch his arms, winced at the sharp reminder of pain and put his hands behind his head instead, so that he didn't grab the smaller man's hips and thrust hard. Stephen's slow movements meant Crane had only half penetrated him yet, and his balls were painfully tight with the need to fill his lover the rest of the way. He bit his lip.

"Are you suffering, my lord?" enquired Stephen softly, feathering kisses over his chest. "Tell me what you want."

"You're in charge."

Stephen paused and tweaked a nipple punitively. "Yes, and I told you to tell me what you want. I like the way you talk to me."

Crane groaned. "Christ, Stephen. I want you to fuck yourself on me. Pleasure yourself on my cock exactly how you want. Make yourself come."

"Oh God, yes," Stephen said, and sank down to take Crane to the hilt in one smooth rush. Crane cried out in time with his lover's low moan, and Stephen began to fuck in earnest.

His hands were fiery on Crane's shoulders, the borrowed tattoo shrieking soundlessly on his pale skin, as he moved with concentrated deliberation, pulling up till only the head of Crane's cock was in him and then thrusting downwards to take him deep. His own prick was glistening and iron hard against Crane's stomach, and Crane said hoarsely, "Tell me if I can touch you."

"No. I want to come like this. Just from you."

Crane's breath rasped. Stephen hissed, changed the angle, and threw his head back. "*Yes.* Is this good for you, Lucien? Do you need to move?"

"I've never been harder," Crane said through his teeth. "And if I move at all, it'll be to throw you on the floor and ravage you like a wild animal, so don't even suggest it."

"I have absolutely no idea who's in charge now," Stephen said breathily. He was moving faster, body tight and tense around Crane's erection.

"You. Always you."

"I'll remind you of that when you've got me chained to the bed."

"You won't need to," Crane said, feeling Stephen's hands pulse against him, his straining prick swelling as he rode him harder and harder. "Not that you'll be able to talk for my cock in your mouth, of course. In your mouth, in your sweet arse, taking my pleasure and making you come till you're sobbing for mercy, because that's exactly how you like it, and I will always give you exactly what you want—"

"*Lucien!*" shrieked Stephen, and climaxed violently, splashing hot against Crane's belly, and rocking with an uncoordinated abandon that brought Crane off just a few strokes later.

They clutched each other, gasping and whispering broken words of love and lust as the tattooed magpies fluttered back and forth between them.

"There's one on your neck," Stephen observed, when he had his breath back. "It looks like you've never shaved. Go, on, shoo." He waved a hand at the wandering tattoo, urging it down.

"Bloody birds," said Crane, watching an inky beak peck at Stephen's nipple. "No, actually, I take that back."

"So you should. I'm becoming increasingly fond of them, the more they save our skins."

"Pure self-interest on their part." Crane stroked a finger along the fine lines at the corner of Stephen's eye, the marks of too many things that couldn't be unseen. "Are you all right, sweet boy? That was what you needed?"

Stephen tipped his head, considering thoughtfully. "Yes. I think it was, actually. Thank you."

"For God's sake!" Crane began, and then caught the glint in Stephen's eye and dumped a scoop of water over him, in lieu of rebuke. Stephen retaliated by sending a wave of water from the basin, drenching Crane completely. Laughing, they washed again, and finally wandered through to the kitchen to raid the larder. Stephen perched naked on the kitchen table as Crane sliced him a wedge of bread and ham.

"What will you do now?" Stephen asked, once he'd devoured half of it.

"Right now? Take you to bed and keep you there till tomorrow lunchtime, at least. Longer term? Move my trading operations here, I think. If I'm staying—and I am—I'll need to shift the control across and appoint a factor who'll only steal with one hand, not both. I can build up the European side of things a fair bit, which might be interesting. And I ought to take the Vaudrey estates more seriously as well. I've repaired some of my father's idiocy but there's a lot more to be done. And my cousins are becoming a bloody nuisance, which needs dealing with. I won't be short of work."

"Sometimes I'm very glad I'm poor," Stephen said. "Would you also have time to act as a liaison with the Chinese, at least for a while? There's doubtless chaos brewing in Limehouse with the remaining shamans, and I need someone I can trust to work with us."

"Will Mrs. Gold be happy with that?"

"I think we have her blessing, yes."

"In that case, I'm at your command."

"So you tell me," said Stephen, eyes warm with affection. "Not always, though, I hope."

"Certainly not. If you want to take charge of the fucking again, you can damned well save my life to earn it."

"Now, wait a moment. That means I'm already owed at least three more—"

Crane raised his voice in mock protest and grabbed for him, and they laughed and struggled, while outside the windows and on the roof, the magpies circled and gathered and landed in their hundreds.

Thanks for reading! Please read on for a bonus Charm of Magpies story, *A Case of Spirits*.

A CASE OF SPIRITS

With thanks to Simon, gin guru.

CHAPTER ONE

The weather broke one late August night, the sultry heat that had lain across England like a quilt for months finally giving way to torrential autumn rain that drummed on the dry roofs and baked pavements and desiccated earth of London. It was monsoon rain, the kind that fell in huge, juicy droplets and moved in warm sheets of water through the dusty air. It felt like home.

Crane lay in bed, listening to the hard spatter of rain against glass. He had always loved the rainy season in Shanghai. (Merrick hated it, grumbling relentlessly that the whole point of not being in sodding England was you didn't get the sodding rain.) It would be raining there now, and he was aware of a longing for the city he loved, for the monsoon parties, on a barge with the rain drumming on a canopy above, or crammed into some sweaty drinking den, the smell of long-dry stone wetted by the splat of raindrops, and of spices and wet leather. It was all a damned sight more entertaining than England.

But Shanghai would lack Stephen.

His lover was curled against him, deep in sleep. In the moonlight through the half-open curtains, Crane could see the borrowed magpie tattoo rustling its wings on his pale skin, still magically animated after the night's lovemaking. He let his hand hover over Stephen's back and watched the inked bird mime a peck at his fingers.

"Stay," he told the tattoo softly. He hadn't chosen to inflict it on Stephen, and would not have volunteered to sacrifice it if he'd been consulted, but he liked to see it there all the same. Stephen felt branded by it, he knew, marked as his, and Crane took a pleasure in the thought that slightly disturbed him. *My lover. My shaman. My bloody-minded, obstinate, slippery Stephen.*

He could live with England for Stephen. But still, he lay sleepless, listening to the rain and thinking of Shanghai.

The scrape and muffled bang of the back door came as a relief. If he wasn't going to sleep, he could at least talk to Merrick. He was in the mood for reminiscence and, judging by the unusually loud sounds from the end of the flat, scraping chairs and a heavy thump, Merrick had been out on the lash. A last late drink might be amusing. Crane extricated himself with care from Stephen's unconscious embrace, padded across the floor to pick up one of his Chinese silk gowns, and slipped out of the bedroom.

The door to the kitchen was closed. He pulled it open, to see the kitchen illuminated by a single candle and Merrick slumped on a chair, head in hands. He was beginning a sarcastic remark on the topic of inebriated wastrels when Merrick jerked upright in his seat and said, "Did you see him?"

"Who?" enquired Crane, shutting the door behind himself and wrinkling his nose at the whiff of strong spirits. "Christ, you've been hitting it a bit hard, haven't you? Where've you been?"

"Old Tom." Merrick slurred the words.

Crane found himself slightly annoyed that he was so ill acquainted with London's lowest drinking dens that he didn't recognise the name. In Shanghai he'd have known where Merrick had been, would probably have drunk there with him. "Who were you out with?"

Merrick's eyes were unfocused. His face worked for a second. "Mr. Humphris."

That must have been a mishearing. "Humphreys? Who's that, one of your disreputable associates?"

"Humphris," Merrick rasped, and Crane did not mishear him that time. The reminder of poor dead Monk was unwelcome.

"All right, not amusing. You should get to bed."

Merrick wasn't listening. He slowly lifted a hand, pointing at Crane. His finger shook.

"Oh for God's sake. You're rat-arsed. What are you doing?"

"*Behind you.*"

Crane didn't even look round. He flung himself forward and sideways, lunging for a knife from the work surface as he moved, and brought it up and out, ready to strike, even as he turned and saw—

Nothing. A closed door. No threat at all. As if there would have been anything to fear in his own flat.

"Cretin." He slapped the knife down, irritated by his own reaction, and turned back to his man. Merrick was still staring, mouth forming soundless words. His eyes were wide, dark pits in the dim light.

Seeing things that weren't there was Stephen's job. "What have you been drinking? Come on, you bloody fool, up."

"Mr. Humphris," Merrick whispered. "He's there."

Crane couldn't stop himself from glancing round again. Too much time with Stephen: the most bizarre statements sounded plausible. "He's not there. You're drunk."

"Stocking round his throat. Oh Christ. He's looking at you."

"All right, that'll do." Crane tugged at Merrick's arm, meaning to get him on his feet, and as he did, Merrick lunged for his shoulder, jerking him off balance. Crane had to grab the table to prevent himself from being pulled to the floor. "The fuck—"

"*Wugu!*"

Crane ducked behind the table, and immediately swore, at Merrick and himself. *Wugu*, evil magic, had played a large part in their lives since their return to England, and they had at least one powerful warlock enemy still at large. He didn't want to be reminded of that in his own home.

He tried to stand, only to be pushed down by the hand on his shoulder. "Get off. There's nothing there and we are both too old for this idiocy. You're going to bed."

Merrick didn't reply, but the fingers on Crane's shoulder changed their grip, no longer pushing him out of range of nonexistent threats, but digging in, holding on, as if desperate for support. "Yuan-yuan," he said hoarsely. "She's here. She's here."

"Oh Jesus." Crane twisted so he could grab Merrick's arm. "Stop it. I'm here, she's not. There's nobody there. Are you listening to me?"

"I see her." Merrick's face was white as he stared into the middle distance. "I see the baby. *I can see them all.*"

Crane grabbed his jaw, pulling his head round, ready to shout in his face, but the words withered on his lips.

Merrick's eyes were liquid. No pupil, no iris, no whites. Just viscous, clear fluid, faintly tinged with shifting swirls of grey and blue, and as Crane stared, a single drop of it rolled out, tearlike, from one eye and trickled down his cheek.

"Stephen!" he roared, lunging for the door and pulling it open. *"Stephen!"*

Stephen was already out of bed and stumbling across the room, naked, bleary and mumbling, as Crane reached the bedroom door. Crane grabbed his wrist and hauled him bodily into the kitchen, almost pushing him at Merrick. "Look at his fucking eyes. Do something."

"Hell's teeth." Stephen snapped into full awareness in the two strides it took to reach the table. He grabbed Merrick's face, hands searching. "What happened?"

"I don't know. He's drunk as a lord and seeing ghosts—oh Christ." Merrick's eyes were bulging now, as if the clear stuff was in a bag that someone was squeezing. More of the thick tears were spilling out. His mouth was working. "Make it *stop.*"

Stephen's face was intent. "Trying. This isn't external, there's no equivalency, this is some kind of…what in the world…"

Merrick made a strangled noise. "Vaudrey."

"I'm here," Crane said, but Merrick didn't seem to be talking to him.

"Vaudrey. Idiot. Fucking barbarian. I got you out!" The horrible stuff in his eyes pulsed wildly, and then, with a sudden jerk, he slumped back in his chair, head lolling.

"*Merrick!*"

"No, it's fine." Stephen moved behind Merrick's chair to put his hands on the unconscious man's skull, frowning down. "Well, it's not, but that was me knocking him out. I don't think he should be conscious. Whatever's going on is happening from inside him, and it's not good. Can you get me something to wear?"

"Is he going to be all right?"

"I don't know what's wrong."

Crane clenched his fists. "I need you to help him."

"Let me work, Lucien. And clothes, *please*."

Crane wouldn't have considered it cold, didn't give a damn if it was, with Merrick sprawled unconscious and that thick, sticky tear sliding over his jaw, but Stephen didn't have a lot of padding on his slim frame. He fetched another of his Chinese dressing gowns—they were ludicrously long on Stephen, smothering him with silk; at another time he would have appreciated the sight—and dropped it over his shoulders. Stephen didn't respond. He was locked in thought, utterly absorbed, and Crane wanted to shake him until he gave some answers.

He waited as long as he could, perhaps a minute, before demanding, "Anything?"

"Hard to say." Stephen's hands were moving over and around Merrick's face, twitching and plucking at the air. "What did you mean, he was seeing ghosts?"

"He said he could see Monk Humphris. And his wife."

"Mr. Humphris's wife?"

"Merrick's."

Stephen looked up, startled. "I didn't know he was married. What happened to her?"

Crane's lungs felt tight and airless. It was a long time since he had spoken of this. "She died in labour. Ten years ago. He, ah, he said he saw the baby."

"The child died too?"

It was one of Crane's worst memories, from a wide selection. The screams, the midwife's bloody hands, her flat demand that Merrick decide whether they should try to save mother or child. His face as he chose, and again, later, as it became clear that his decision had been wrong, or perhaps that it had always been meaningless.

Afterwards, when it was over, they had crawled into a bottle for days. Then Crane had hauled him out of Shanghai on a rambling trading trip that lasted a year or more, its only purpose to be moving, always moving.

Stephen was nodding, evidently reading the answer in his face. "And you?"

"What about me?"

"He saw you. Something about a barbarian, he didn't get you out. What was that?"

Crane's hand went up, involuntarily, to the back of his neck. He wouldn't have been surprised to feel that the thin cuts, long since healed and faded, had reopened. It felt that raw tonight. "The warlord, in the north. Where we were when Xan Ji-yin got himself killed. He was a big sod called Boghda and I had a few highly enjoyable months with him, and then...it became less enjoyable and he, uh, confined me to his rooms when I tried to leave. It took Merrick a few weeks to get me away from there. But he did get me out. I'm not a ghost."

The doorbell jangled in the front hall, making them both jump. Crane glared at the clock, which showed half past midnight. "Who the hell is that?"

"Can you get it?" Stephen was intent on Merrick again. Crane strode into the pitch-black hallway and immediately barked his shins on some damn table or other. He fumbled for a lamp and turned on the gas with the usual hiss and foul odour. "Light," he called back to Stephen.

The gas ignited obediently, and Crane hurried to the heavy front door, pulling it open as the doorbell pealed again, to see Esther Gold. She looked pallid. Her hair was twisted into a chaotic, tangled knot and her dress had several dark wet patches on the skirts. "Lord Crane. I'm hoping you have Stephen here."

She was not taking Stephen from Merrick, no matter the crisis. "He's busy."

"He's about to be busier." She pushed past Crane without ceremony. "Steph!"

"Kitchen," came Stephen's abstracted voice. "I've a problem here."

"Is it seeing ghosts?"

Crane grabbed her shoulder. She turned with a warning glare that he ignored. "Do you know about this?"

"Not to say *know*." Esther shrugged him off a little too easily, and hurried forward, scowling as she saw the dimly lit scene in the kitchen. A couple of candles flared to life. "Is that Mr. Merrick? Did you put him out before his eyes burst?"

"*What?*"

"Yes, I thought things might be going that way." Stephen sounded far too calm. "What's happening?"

"We've nine—now ten—victims shouting about seeing people who aren't there. Their eyes go clear and viscous, and if they keep watching—" She flicked her fingers open, making a popping noise with her lips. "It's hellish messy, we have no idea what it is, and, Steph…it's got Saint."

Stephen's head jerked up at that. "Is she—"

"I knocked her out in time."

Stephen's face was closing into his implacable professional expression, the cold point where justice became retribution. His voice was level as he said, "I don't think it's ghosts. Mr. Merrick saw Lord Crane."

"What circumstances?"

"Leaving him in trouble." The two justiciars exchanged glances, in apparent mutual understanding, and Stephen shrugged slightly. "Let's find out. I'll, uh, get dressed. Is there anything I can do for him now, Es?"

"Not that I know of. Put him in bed and make sure he won't wake."

"Is that safe, leaving him?" Crane demanded.

"I'll keep him unconscious," Stephen said. "He won't wake and as far as I can tell he won't worsen. There's nothing else we can do to help him except find out what's happening and put a stop to it."

Crane nodded. "Are you sure that this is general? Not an attack on Merrick, or me through him?"

"There's nine more victims out there," Esther said. "Including a lawyer, Saint, assorted costers, two ladies of the night, one schoolteacher and a sexton. It looks random."

"Do I need to stay with him?"

"Do you have other plans?" Esther enquired.

"I don't think there's anything much to be gained from staying, if there's somewhere you need to be," Stephen said. "He won't know any different. I can ward the doors, if you come out now. Er, where are you going?"

"I'm coming with you."

Stephen frowned. "Lucien, I don't think—"

"This thing made him see Yuan-yuan." Crane heard the thick anger in his own voice. "So you are going to identify who did it, and make it stop, and then I am going to twist the fu—the *individual*'s head off his shoulders. Slowly."

"I think my sensibilities can cope with that," said Esther. "Come if you want. I don't care, as long as you hurry."

CHAPTER TWO

Esther had a cab waiting to take them eastwards to Seething Lane and the little medieval church that stood there. Lights burned inside, flickering through the windows, and Crane could hear cries and moans as he hurried inside, out of the downpour.

"It's all happening in this area, so we're gathering the victims here," Esther told Stephen, leading the way to the door. "Their sexton was one of the first. Dan's in there. Macready's team and Janossi are on the street, trying to pick up any new ones before their eyes go."

Inside, the church was chaos. A row of five bodies on the floor looked appalling but, Crane realised, those must be the unfortunates found and rendered unconscious in time. The rest of them... He set his teeth at the sight. They huddled together, hands waving and groping, empty eye sockets dark-red pits in faces stained with glistening tracks. The air was filled with wailing, a choir of high, persistent shrieks and the low throb of hard, choking sobs. The church stank of wet clothes, filthy bodies and cheap drink. A vicar was clutching the hand of a neatly dressed woman, still with her bonnet pinned to her head, as she rocked back and forth, wailing. A few men and women wearing green sashes were moving around with cups of tea and blankets. Dr. Daniel Gold was in the middle of the crowd, curly hair wild, in savage argument with a red-faced man in a black suit and slippers. Crane recognised the nurse from Gold's surgery, wiping clear slime from the thin, ravaged face of a child of no more than seven.

Esther and Stephen headed off without a word. Crane, lacking a purpose, went over to Gold and the crowd of sufferers, trying not to focus on the ruined faces. His imagination was painting Merrick with those awful empty pits in place of his bright, knowing hazel eyes, and it made his stomach turn. He set his jaw.

Gold was glowering into the slippered man's face. "I don't give a damn. I need *help*. I need nurses, I need supplies—"

"And who's going to pay for that?" demanded the man. "This parish barely keeps its doors open as it is. We don't have the money for doctors. *You* brought all these people here—"

"And now they need help."

"Not at our expense!"

Gold's face tightened with anger. "How remarkably Christian."

"That will do." Crane put savage command into the words, making both combatants jump. "I'll pay for whatever you need. Get it now. Lord Crane," he added to the slippered man before he could ask. "No expense to be spared, now do as the doctor says. Move!"

Gold had already grabbed his nurse and launched into a rapid stream of instructions. Crane hovered till it was clear he was not needed, then took a pew and leaned forward, staring at his hands, until he heard voices near him.

"I said, sit *down*, Doctor." It was the nurse from Gold's surgery, pushing him towards a pew. "Ten minutes off your feet before you fall over. Tea, please," she called across the room.

Crane shifted up, making room for the doctor to sit by him. Daniel Gold looked exhausted, clothes stained with thick, glistening ichor, and Crane tried not to wince as he rubbed a dirty hand through his hair.

"Lord Crane. Thank you for that. For the money, and for making me stop talking. It's been the devil of a night." Gold shut his eyes and tipped his head back. "Did Esther say this thing's got Saint?"

"And Merrick."

"Oh Lord. I'm sorry. Ah, his eyes—?"

"Stephen knocked him out in time." There was a piercing shriek from the crowd of sufferers. Crane winced. "For Christ's sake, why don't you do something about them? Knock them out too?"

"To what end?" asked Gold. "They'll still wake up blind. And we need to try and get some kind of coherent answers from them, I'm afraid, perhaps even see if we can find out what's going on through them. I'm sorry for the poor devils, but the priority is to save those who have a chance yet."

Crane gritted his teeth. "What's happened here, Doctor?"

"Drink," said a woman loudly from beside the pew. She had a green sash slung across her body and was holding a tray with tin mugs of steaming tea. Gold passed one to Crane and took one for himself. "The demon drink. They swill it down till it sends them blind. This is what comes of a man reducing himself to an ape, or a devil." Her face was lit with righteous anger. "All the evils of London spring from the curse of alcohol."

"We're both teetotal," Gold assured her. "Lifelong. They need more tea over there, please." He gestured at the furthest possible end of the church and gave her an expectant look until she went away.

Crane sipped his tea and made a face at the stewed tannic taste. Gold gave a wry smile. "The brew that cheers, but not inebriates, unfortunately. Although I shouldn't say that too loudly, the place is crawling with abstainers. They do good work here, but it comes with a heavy dose of righteousness."

"The green-sash people? Who are they?" Crane didn't care in the slightest, but conversation was a distraction from the background noise, and his thoughts.

Gold looked as though he felt the same. "Temperance Society. Set of fanatics. They march all over town, picketing public houses, making a nuisance of themselves to decent publicans and moonshiners alike. I had one turn up in my surgery. She got in posing as a patient and then started lecturing me about the use of rubbing alcohol. Which, let it be said, I almost never drink." Gold rubbed at his face again. "They have a point, of course, the curse of the labouring classes and all that. But I could use a glass of something now."

"Or a bottle. What *is* this thing, Doctor?"

"I have no idea. It acts between the body and the mind, that's all I'm sure of. We've been checking the unconscious ones and their eyes are still, ah, *wrong*, but not bursting."

"Will you be able to heal them?" The tin sides of the mug bowed slightly under Crane's tight grip. The painful heat was welcome.

Gold gestured helplessly. "I need to know what it was and how it works, and I don't know anything. Look at the victims: the sexton, a schoolteacher, whores, a child, Saint. Respectable people and the worst sort. All ages. What the devil do they have in common?"

"None of them have said anything about what happened?"

"The ones who aren't unconscious or screaming are still undergoing whatever it is. We're having trouble getting past what's going on in their minds. And it doesn't help that two-thirds of them are drunk as lords, no offence intended."

"It would hardly do to say blind drunk," Crane retorted.

Gold's lips twisted. "Indeed not. It's probably a blessing for the incapables, actually. I wouldn't want to be sober if I were them." He rolled his shoulders. "I should get back to work. Talking of which, how much of your money can I spend?"

"Anything you need." Crane did not intend to hold desperate hands or apply dressings to empty eye sockets, but this was a contribution he could make, some small offering to the Fates for Merrick's sake. "Hire everyone you need, and find a damned cure for this."

"We're doing our best." Gold drained his mug, put it on the pew in front and rubbed at his unpleasantly stained sleeve. "God, this is foul stuff. Right, excuse me. Oh, it's you," he added, looking over Crane's shoulder. "I suppose you want my seat."

"I do," Stephen said, and collapsed on the pew in Gold's place as the doctor went back to the fray. "Is that tea?"

"Nominally." Crane passed him the mostly untouched mug. "Have you got any idea what's happening?"

Stephen took a swig, winced, and shook his head. "We think they've been poisoned. Don't know where, how or why. There's no common thread between the victims, except that most of them turned up within a mile or so of here. None of them are able to talk properly, so we aren't having much luck asking."

"You can't fluence them?"

Stephen flicked him a look. Crane shrugged. He did not want his own mind tampered with; other people's minds were of a great deal less value to him than Merrick's eyes.

"We don't think it's safe to try. Goodness knows what we might do to them if we start playing about with their minds now."

As if Crane gave a damn for them. He stared at his interlocked fingers, quivering with helpless rage that needed a target. Stephen put a hand on his arm, a light touch, nothing that would attract attention, and Crane had to bite back a surge of fury that he could not turn and hold on to him. He wanted to take some comfort from his lover, to stave off the fear and horror, but to do so was only to face a different threat, one that was clearly in Stephen's mind even now.

"Let's not forget discretion." He jerked his arm to shake Stephen's hand off altogether, a twitch of anger at bloody England, bloody magic, bloody enigmatic shamans, that mostly spited himself.

Stephen looked startled, and a little hurt. He pressed his lips together, keeping his patience. "Dan said you're bankrolling him. Thank you."

"My pleasure. It allows me to pretend I'm not completely powerless."

Stephen watched him a moment longer, then finished his tea with a grimace. "You don't have any idea at all where Mr. Merrick spent the evening? If I could start looking somewhere—"

"Yes." Crane cursed himself that he hadn't thought of it. "He told me he'd been somewhere called the Old Tom. Do you know it?"

Stephen had sat up straight at Crane's reply. Now he sagged back slightly. "There's no such place."

"He definitely said—"

"No, I mean, it's a general name. An Old Tom is a house, or shop, or even a public house, that sells cheap moonshine gin. Going back to when gin was illegal. If there's a carving or plaque of a black cat out the front, that's an Old Tom. Knock on the window, pay your penny and get your poison."

"Are there many of these places left?" Crane asked without much hope. "Since gin is now readily obtainable in public houses."

"A fair few. They're much cheaper, for good reason, Lord only knows what you end up drinking. Dan's always telling Saint not to—" He stopped short.

Crane felt his skin prickle. "Not to…?"

"Dan tells Saint not to go to them," Stephen said slowly. "But she very often does. On her night off."

"Was it her night off tonight?"

"It was. Mr. Merrick went to an Old Tom tonight too. And because they're very cheap—"

"They're attractive to costers and children and whores." Crane twisted round to look at the little group of sufferers. "And a knock at a window is much more discreet than entering a public house if you're a schoolmistress or a lawyer—"

"Or a sexton at a temperance church." Stephen was on his feet. "Esther? Es! We've got something."

Esther agreed that it was the best lead they had. The problem was, it didn't lead anywhere.

"I don't *know* these places." Frustration rang in Stephen's voice. "We need a list, all of them within, I don't know, a mile of here. Saint would know, that's the damned thing. Maybe if we went to the police they could come up with something, if we can find someone at this hour—"

"Hold on." There was one of the green-sashed campaigners bustling by. Crane put out a hand to detain her. "Excuse me, madam. Do you assist in the work of the Temperance Society?"

"I do." She drew herself up, pose challenging.

"I'm delighted to hear it. My name is Lord Crane, I'm an abstainer myself and I heartily support your cause." Stephen's face in his peripheral vision was entirely blank. "We need, urgently, to know where the Old Toms in this area are. It's possible they may be at the root of this business."

"I knew it!" Her eyes lit up. "The curse of drink—"

"Absolutely, yes, but do you know them?"

She gave a self-conscious bob, and Crane regretted using his title. "Well—that is, my lord, you understand that we are forced to go to the most disreputable places—"

"You can't fight the good fight without knowing your enemy," Crane assured her. In the background, Esther was starting to twitch. "I have nothing but the greatest respect for your courage and dedication, now give me addresses. Please."

She preened just a little. "There's a house on Crutched Friars, and two on Fenchurch Street. Leadenhall Street, and Mincing Lane."

Esther was scrawling on a bit of paper. Stephen looked appalled. "That many?"

The lady drew herself up to lecture. Crane said, "Please go on," before she could start.

"Great Tower Street, and Idol Lane. *There's* a suitable address for the worship of inebriation. Unlike Rood Lane."

"Was that Rood Lane or not?" Esther asked, scribbling.

"We won a victory over the devil there." The lady glowed with pride. "A poison peddler, sinner and drunkard, now turned from his evil ways by the grace of God."

"Congratulations," Crane said. "More names."

She rattled off half a dozen more streets. Stephen enquired, carefully, "Do you have any reason to believe any of these, er, poison peddlers were involved in other forms of evil? Dark arts?"

The temperance crusader, looking slightly taken aback, denied all knowledge of such things and had nothing else of use to offer.

"What now?" Crane asked.

"I suppose we'll have to go and look at them. Coming?" Stephen led the way to the door.

Crane followed, grabbing his overcoat. "There must be fifteen addresses there. Where do we start?"

"Rood Lane," the justiciars chorused.

Crane frowned. "I thought she said the Rood Lane one was closed down."

"We have a rule of thumb," Stephen said. "Always start with the fanatics."

They walked, since there were no cabs to be had and it was only a few hundred yards. The rain had slackened off and the streets were a little fresher smelling for it. Small groups lurked in doorways, watching the passersby. Crane doubted they'd be troubled. They might look on the face of it like easy pickings, the short man, the rich man, and the woman, but purpose rang in the justiciars' strides and showed in their faces. You would have to be suicidal to cross Esther or Stephen tonight, but Crane almost hoped someone would try. He needed a target.

As they turned onto Rood Lane, Esther's head reared back and she gave a deep, rattling sniff. "Oh yes. Down here." She lengthened her stride, sniffing again.

Crane glanced at Stephen. He shrugged. "My hands, her nose. She's rarely wrong."

Esther halted outside a nondescript house, its windows closed for the night with wooden shutters. Crane could just make out the faded caricature of a black cat by the side of the door. There was no light showing. Crane knocked to no effect.

Esther tried the door and found it locked. She put both hands flat on the wood and leaned forward, head resting against it for a moment, then stepped away. "Kick that for me, Lord Crane. It should be quite easy."

"That's not very subtle," Stephen observed.

"I don't feel very subtle."

"Nor I." Crane measured the distance and launched a savage kick at the solid oak, which gave way like sodden paper. He had to grab the doorframe to stop himself from falling through after it.

It was dark and cold inside the house, and it smelled of spirits and herbs—rosemary, juniper. The volatile fumes caught at Crane's nostrils and seared along his breath as he inhaled. "Do we want to smell this?"

Light bloomed to his side, and he saw Stephen, face illuminated by a yellow glow that spread from his hands, upwards and out.

"You mentioned subtlety," Esther said dryly.

"It's a bit late for that."

They headed up the stairs, just as a scrawny man appeared on the landing, nightshirt flapping around bony legs. "What the bloody hell?" he spluttered. "Get out! I'll call the law!"

"We are the law," Stephen said. "Let's talk about drink."

CHAPTER THREE

They sat downstairs, surrounding the man, who gave his name as Steel. He looked cold. Neither justiciar put a light to the fireplace. A green sash hung over the back of a chair.

Steel huddled in his chair, guilty but defiant. He had rheumy eyes, spidery traces of broken blood vessels across his cheeks, calloused knuckles that had seen much use. He might have stopped drinking; he still looked like a drunk.

"I hate drinkers," he mumbled. "Filthy animals. I was an animal, in my cups. Drink is a curse."

Esther rolled her eyes. "So we've heard. Tell us what you did."

"I used my great-aunt's book. She made all sorts. Had her own still, brewed special ales. Some of her drinks, they…did things. Well, I found a recipe, a gin called Remembrance. A drink to bring back memories, she said it was."

"Why did you want to bring back memories?" Stephen asked.

"You ever hear of drinking to forget?" Steel spat on the floor. "They ought to remember. Drink is a sin, and worse sin comes from it. They ought to feel their shame, be made to feel it. *I* feel my shame. I did terrible things under the influence." He was looking at Esther as he spoke, eyes glinting. "Terrible things. I'm the lowest and worst of sinners—"

"Yes," Stephen said, the single word cutting Steel off before he could launch into an obviously well-used recitation. "I'd like to see this book now."

"It's mine."

Esther folded her arms. "Mr. Steel, are you aware of what your gin actually does to people?"

"Makes them remember. That's what the book said."

"Did you test it, on anything or anyone—yourself, perhaps— before you started doling it out?"

Steel looked blank. "No."

"You distilled liquor to what must have been quite an unusual recipe, and then you served it to people, without any effort to find out what it would do." Esther sounded very mild, in the way that presaged explosions.

"It's God's work. Drink is a sin."

"So is poisoning people." Stephen's voice was level, far too level. Crane looked from his face to Esther's and fought an instinctive urge to step back. "Even if all it did was bring back memories, you had no right to make that judgement. As it is, Mr. Steel, you have blood on your hands."

"Or some sort of fluid, at least." Esther's smile was entirely humourless. "I think we'll take you with us. You can see what you've achieved in the name of temperance. I'm sure you'll be very proud."

"They came to me for it! They knocked on the window, paid their pennies." Steel looked at all three faces, seeking understanding. "They'd have grovelled in the gutter for it if they hadn't had it from me. They wanted their drink, and I gave it them. As they deserved."

"Hold on," Crane said. "You're an abstainer in the temperance movement, but you sell gin?"

Steel gave him a baffled look. "Well? Man's got to make a living."

"And on that note…" Stephen stood. "You will now give us any remaining Remembrance gin, and the book."

Steel stuck out his jaw. "What if I don't?"

Stephen sighed. "You can hand them over now, or you can hand them over with broken bones and missing teeth after Lord Crane has taken his feelings out on you for five minutes. I don't care which."

"Really? I have a strong preference." Crane stood, and saw Steel's eyes widen. He smiled at the huddled man and took a single step forward.

Esther tutted. "I cannot possibly witness such a disgusting spectacle." She rose. "Which gives Mr. Steel until I reach the door to decide."

Two hours later, they sat together on a pew, Stephen's shoulder warm against Crane's side.

They had dragged Steel back to St. Olave's, Esther marching him along while Crane carried a jug of the Remembrance gin, and Stephen clutched an ancient book tightly to stop bits of herbs and parchment falling out of it. Steel had argued and protested all the way, until Esther shoved him towards the group of whimpering, eyeless victims, showed him the blinded child, told him what he had done. The temperance crusaders had taken him away after that. Crane didn't care. He wanted to step on the man as he would a roach, but it would be a distraction, and the practitioners were busy.

There had been running and shouting. Several hastily summoned people had appeared, in garments ranging from dressing gowns to ball gowns, and there had been a lot of huddled argument over the gin bottle and the recipe book, with Dan Gold in the middle of it. Esther and Stephen had darted around the edge of the crowd, keeping order in a way that reminded Crane irresistibly of sheepdogs. And at last Stephen had emerged from the fray to flop down on the hard seat next to him.

"They're looking for some sort of solution," he said without preamble. "The recipe was clear. Far too clear. Someone should have made sure that book was destroyed when its owner died. Talk about falling into the wrong hands."

"So, is Steel a practitioner?"

"A flit." Stephen made a sour face. "A tiny bit of talent, just enough to ensure that it worked, without any idea what he was doing. Damned fool. He'll be dealt with."

"And…the solution?" Crane made himself ask the question that had been sitting, sickeningly, in his gut for hours. "Can you save their eyes? Merrick's eyes?"

"We've managed to stop the blinded ones from remembering, so they're no longer seeing ghosts. It's a good start."

"That's not what I asked. Damn it—" Crane's voice rose. He could not tolerate Stephen's habitual evasion now.

"Look there." Stephen nodded to where Dan Gold and a bespectacled woman, incongruous and magnificent in red satin, crouched by the row of unconscious victims. "That's Mrs. Baron Shaw. She's on the Council. She was at a party with the Prince of Wales tonight. We dragged her away from waltzing with royalty at some glittering soiree to come here because she's the best at unpicking this kind of mess. If she and Dan can't do it between them, then no, it won't be possible." He looked up at Crane. "I know you're frightened. I know you hate this, and you want me to make it stop. I'm sure you'd rather that I was doing something spectacular to fix it, and so would I, but that's not always within my powers." His amber eyes were deeply serious. "I'm not making you promises I can't keep. I will never do that."

He held Crane's gaze until, finally, Crane gave him an acknowledging nod. "I know."

"It's Saint's sight too."

"I know. I'm sorry."

Stephen sighed. "The young fool that she is. How on earth did they both end up drinking at the same Old Tom?"

"God knows." Merrick had been on the lash with the young justiciar a couple of times since the rat business. Crane didn't intend to share that information with Stephen right now. Instead, he leaned back, stretching his long legs under the pew in front, appallingly tired and uncomfortable. "So, now we wait."

"Afraid so." Stephen was silent for long enough that Crane felt startled when he asked, "What would you see?"

"Sorry?"

"If you drank the gin. I was just thinking. Ghosts, memories, regrets."

"Christ, what a question." Crane hesitated. "I don't know. A houseful of ghosts, probably. I've a lot of memories I wouldn't want to be confronted with. But as to regrets… They don't mean much. You do what you can at the time, and if you fail, you learn. Apparently Merrick thinks he let me down not getting me away from the warlord fast enough. I can tell you, I feel nothing but pure bloody relief that he got me out at all."

"Yes. I see."

"In any case, my life has brought me here, with you, and I wouldn't want to be elsewhere." The knot of anger that had roiled inside him for hours loosened a little as Crane felt the truth of his own words. He could not have borne this without Stephen, without the knowledge, under his own helpless fury, that his quiet, determined, implacable lover was there, fighting for him once again. "Although I'd rather not be sitting on this damned uncomfortable pew, of course."

Stephen smiled up at that. "You're good at living in the present, aren't you?"

"Is there a choice?"

There was, suddenly, a pressure against his fingers. It was like a hand, but with none of Stephen's electric touch, and neither warm nor cold. He glanced down, startled, and saw nothing. Stephen's hands were demurely folded on his lap.

"Is that you?"

"It is." The invisible clasp firmed, stroking his skin.

"That's giving me ideas."

Stephen's eyes widened. "Not in a church, Lucien."

"I'll have ideas anywhere I damned well please."

Stephen grinned, settling back. Crane watched his face, the thin lines of strain around his eyes, and remarked, "You'd have a fair few ghosts yourself."

"Yes." Stephen was silent for a moment. Crane had not expected more of an answer, and was a little surprised to hear him speak again. "At least there's one I wouldn't have."

"Sorry?"

"I'm glad I didn't walk away from you, back in spring. I'm glad we had our chance. I love you, Lucien." It was quiet, but it was spoken, aloud. Stephen's invisible fingers stroked over his. "And I'm glad I'm with you now. Especially since I'm quite sure you'd haunt me horribly if I weren't."

"To the grave." Crane said it lightly, but he felt Stephen push closer against him, and it was doubtless risky but the church was full of sleepers, many slumped against each other, and everyone awake was working, and bugger the lot of them, anyway. To hell with it. Crane put an arm round his shoulder, felt Stephen's tiny wriggle into him, and closed his own eyes.

"Do get up," said Esther from above them, jolting Crane into wakefulness again. "It's dawn, you can't just loll about on pews. We have a cure."

It was raining again, two nights later. Crane sat at the kitchen table, with a bottle of gin in front of him, and three glasses. The smell of spirits was making him nervous, but there was only one way to deal with that.

Merrick sat opposite him, bright hazel eyes on Crane's. "Did I hear you was paying for them poor buggers that went blind?"

Crane shrugged. "Gold's sorted out the help for them, I'm just funding it. Someone has to."

"Yeah. Nasty business, that. Funny sort of doings all round."

"Yes. Of course, you know the most extraordinary part of the whole thing?"

"What?"

"In twenty years, I never suspected you had a conscience."

Merrick growled. "Do I bollocks. Had a skinful, that's all."

He poured them both a substantial shot of gin. Crane eyed his. "I trust this comes from a reputable source."

"Only the best, my lord."

"Keep that in mind for your future excursions." Crane picked up the glass, looking through the liquid. "Is there anything we need to discuss?"

"Don't reckon so."

Dead men, Yuan-yuan, Saint. He cocked a brow, waiting, just in case.

Merrick lifted a shoulder. "Past is past. Bugger all you can do about it."

"True. Trite, but true."

"Well then. Can't sit around thinking about what's done. We got things to be getting on with, you and me. All of us," he added, and tipped a generous measure of gin into the third tumbler.

Crane had heard it too: the rattle of light footsteps that indicated Stephen coming up the back stairs, coming home to him. He lifted his glass. "I'll drink to that."

THE CHARM OF MAGPIES SERIES

Series reading order is as follows

A Charm of Magpies (Stephen Day and Lord Crane)
   The Magpie Lord
   Interlude with Tattoos (short story)
   A Case of Possession
   A Case of Spirits (short story)
   Flight of Magpies
   Feast of Stephen (short story)

Each book is published with its companion story. 'The Smuggler and the Warlord', a very short early story of Crane and Merrick in China, is available free on my website at kjcharleswriter.com.

The Charm of Magpies World
   Jackdaw
   A Queer Trade (Rag and Bone prequel)
   Rag and Bone

These are standalone stories with different couples taking place in the same world. *A Queer Trade* is set in the summer of *A Case of Possession*; *Jackdaw* and *Rag and Bone* are both set in the spring following *Flight of Magpies*.

Stephen and Crane's story concludes in *Flight of Magpies.*

Flight of Magpies
A Charm of Magpies book 3
Danger in the air. Lovers on the brink.

With the justiciary understaffed, a series of horrifying occult murders to be investigated, and a young student flying off the rails, magical law enforcer Stephen Day is under increasing stress. And the strain is starting to show in his relationship with his aristocratic lover, Lord Crane.

Crane chafes at the restrictions of England's laws, and there's a worrying development in the blood-and-sex bond he shares with Stephen. A development that makes a sensible man question if they should be together at all.

Then a devastating loss brings the people he most loves into bitter conflict. Old enemies, new enemies, and unexpected enemies are painting Stephen and Crane into a corner, and the pressure threatens to tear them apart...

BOOKS BY KJ CHARLES

A Charm of Magpies series
The Magpie Lord
A Case of Possession
Flight of Magpies
Jackdaw
A Queer Trade
Rag and Bone

Society of Gentlemen series
The Ruin of Gabriel Ashleigh
A Fashionable Indulgence
A Seditious Affair
A Gentleman's Position

Sins of the Cities series
An Unseen Attraction
An Unnatural Vice
An Unsuitable Heir

Standalone books
Think of England
The Secret Casebook of Simon Feximal
Wanted, a Gentleman

Green Men
Spectred Isle

ABOUT THE AUTHOR

KJ Charles is a writer and editor. She lives in London with her husband, two kids, a garden with quite enough prickly things, and a cat with murder management issues.

Find her at www.kjcharleswriter.com for book info and blogging, on Twitter @kj_charles for daily timewasting and the odd rant, or in her Facebook group, KJ Charles Chat, for sneak peeks and special extras.